Paddington
Takes the Test

Paddington Takes the Test

REVISED EDITION

by Michael Bond
with drawings by Peggy Fortnum

Houghton Mifflin Company
BOSTON 2002

www.houghtonmifflinbooks.com

First American edition published 1980 by Houghton Mifflin Company

Book design by Carol Goldenberg
The text of this book is set in 13/17pt. Sabon.

Library of Congress Cataloging in Publication Data
Bond, Michael.
Paddington takes the test.
Summary: Presents further misadventures in England of the bear from
Darkest Peru in which he takes a driving test, visits a Stately Home, gets a rise,
and takes part in a magic act.
[1. Bears—Fiction. 2. England—Fiction] I. Fortnum, Peggy. II. Title.
PZ7.B6368Pajj 1980 [Fic] 80–16972
ISBN 0–618–18384–1

Printed in the United States of America
QUM 10 9 8 7 6 5 4 3 2 1

Contents

Paddington
Takes the Test

CHAPTER ONE

Paddington at the Wheel

PADDINGTON GAVE THE MAN facing him one of his hardest stares ever. "I've won a bookmark!" he exclaimed hotly. "But I thought it was going to be a Rolls-Royce."

The man fingered his collar nervously. "There must be some mistake," he replied. "The lucky winner of the car has already been presented with it. And the second prize, a weekend for two in Paris, has gone to an Old Age Pensioner in Edinburgh. If you've had a letter from us, then you must be one of the ten thousand runners-

1

up who merely receive bookmarks. I can't think why one wasn't enclosed."

"I'm one of *ten thousand runners-up?*" repeated Paddington, hardly able to believe his ears.

"I'm afraid so." Regaining his confidence, the man began rummaging in one of his desk drawers. "The trouble is," he said meaningly, "so many entrants to competitions don't bother to read the small print. If you care to take another look at our entry form you'll see what I mean."

Paddington took the leaflet and focused his gaze on a picture of a large, sleek, silver-gray car. A chauffeur, standing beside one of the open doors, was flicking an imaginary speck of dust from the upholstery with one of his gloves, while across the bonnet, in large red letters, were the words ALL THIS COULD BE YOURS!

Having slept with an identical picture under his pillow at number thirty-two Windsor Gardens for several weeks, Paddington felt he knew it all by heart. He turned it over and on the back were the self-same instructions for entering the competition, together with an entry form.

"Now look inside," suggested the man.

Paddington did as he was bidden, and as he did so his face fell. He'd been so excited by the picture of the Rolls-Royce he hadn't bothered to look any further, but

as he pulled the pages apart he found it opened out into a larger sheet. On the left-hand side there was a picture of a French Gendarme pointing toward a distant view of the Eiffel Tower, and on the right, under the heading TEN THOUSAND CONSOLATION PRIZES TO BE WON, there was a picture of a bookmark, followed by a lot of writing.

By the end of the page some of the print was so small Paddington began to wish he'd brought his opera glasses with him, but there was no escaping the fact that the bookmark had an all-too-familiar look about it. One exactly like it had arrived that very morning in the envelope containing news of his success.

"I don't think a bookmark is much consolation for not winning a Rolls-Royce!" he exclaimed. "I put *mine* down the waste disposal. I didn't think it was a *prize*."

"Oh, dear!" The man gave a sympathetic cluck as he riffled through a pile of papers on his desk to show the interview was at an end. "How very unfortunate. Still, at least you've had the benefit of eating some of our sun-kissed currants." He opened one of his desk drawers again and took out a packet. "Have some more as a present," he said.

"But I don't even like currants!" exclaimed Paddington bitterly. "And I ate fifteen boxes of them!"

"*Fifteen?*" The man gazed at Paddington with new respect. "May I ask what your slogan was?"

"A currant a day," said Paddington hopefully, "keeps the doctor away."

"In that case," said the man, permitting himself a smile, "you shouldn't require any medical attention for quite a . . ." His voice trailed away as he caught sight of the look Paddington was giving him.

It had taken Paddington a long time to get through fifteen boxes of currants, not to mention think up a suitable slogan into the bargain. And, if the expression on his face was anything to go by, the whole thing had left him in need of *more* medical attention rather than less.

In fact, as he made his way back down the stairs Paddington began to look more and more gloomy. The news that he wasn't after all the proud possessor of a gleaming new motor car was a bitter blow, one made all the worse because he hadn't even wanted it for himself—it had really been intended as a surprise for Mr. Brown.

Mr. Brown's present car was a bit of a sore point in the Brown household. The general feeling at number thirty-two Windsor Gardens was that it ought to have been pensioned off years ago. But Mr. Brown had held on to it because it was hard to find anything large enough to convey the whole of the family, not to mention Paddington and all his belongings, when they went on their outings.

Apart from its age it had a number of drawbacks, one of which was that instead of flashing lights, it relied on illuminated arms to indicate intended changes of direction. It was the failure of one of these arms, when Mr. Brown had been turning into a main road one day, that had attracted the attention of a passing policeman who'd taken his number.

Paddington had been most upset at the time because he'd been sitting alongside Mr. Brown, ready to help out with paw signals when necessary.

The magistrate had had one or two pointed things to

say about drivers who relied on bears for their signals, and much to Mr. Brown's disgust he'd been ordered to retake his driving test.

It was shortly after this disastrous event that Paddington had come across a leaflet in the local supermarket announcing a competition in which the first prize was a car. And it was not just any old car, but a Rolls-Royce. Paddington felt sure that with a car as grand as a Rolls, Mr. Brown couldn't possibly fail his coming test, let alone have any motoring problems ever again.

The competition was sponsored by a well-known brand of currants, and the lady in the supermarket assured Paddington that there had been nothing like it in the dried-fruit world before. When he consulted the leaflet, with the aid of his torch under the bedclothes that night, he could quite see what she meant, for it couldn't have been more simple. All that was required was a suitable slogan to do with currants, together with three packet tops to show that the entry was genuine.

But the thing which really clinched matters for Paddington was the discovery that not only was the result of the competition being announced on the same day that Mr. Brown was due to take his test, but that the firm who were running it occupied a building on the very same street as the Test Center.

Paddington was a great believer in coincidences; some of his best adventures had come about in just such a way—almost as if they had been meant to happen— and after buying some extra packets of currants in order to make doubly sure of success, he lost no time in sending off his entry.

The fact that in the end it had all come to nought was most disappointing, and as he left the building he paused in order to direct a few more hard stares in the direction of the upper floors. Then he collected his shopping basket on wheels from the car park outside and made his way slowly along the road toward the Test Center.

He was much earlier than he had expected to be and so he wasn't too surprised to find Mr. Brown's car still standing where it had been parked earlier that morning. Neither Mr. Brown nor Mrs. Brown was anywhere in sight, and being the sort of bear who didn't believe in wasting time, Paddington parked his shopping basket on wheels alongside it. Then he climbed into the driver's seat and switched on the radio while he awaited developments.

Like the car itself, Mr. Brown's radio had seen better days. It somehow managed to make everything sound the same, rather like an old-fashioned horn gramophone, and in no time at all Paddington found himself

starting to nod off. His eyelids got heavier and heavier and soon the sound of gentle snoring added itself to the music.

Paddington had no idea how long he slept, but he was just in the middle of a very vivid dream in which he was driving down a long road, battling against a storm of currants as big as hailstones, when he woke with a start and found to his surprise that two men were standing outside the car peering through the window at him. One of them was carrying a large clipboard to which was attached a sheaf of very important looking papers, and he was tapping on the glass in no uncertain manner.

Paddington hastily removed his paws from the steering wheel and opened the driver's door.

"Is your name Brown?" demanded the man with the clipboard, trying to make himself heard above the radio. "From number thirty-two Windsor Gardens?"

"That's right," said Paddington, looking most surprised.

"Hmm." The man gave him an odd look and then consulted the papers on his board. "Er . . . I take it you *are* a British subject?" he asked.

Paddington considered the matter for a moment. "Well," he said, "yes and no . . ."

"Yes and no?" repeated the man sharply. "You can't be yes *and* no. You must be one thing or the other."

"I *live* at number thirty-two Windsor Gardens," said Paddington firmly, "but I *come* from Darkest Peru."

"Darkest Peru? Oh!" The man began to look as if he rather wished he hadn't brought the matter up. Hastily changing the subject, he motioned with his free hand toward his companion. "I take it you won't mind if we're accompanied?" he asked. Then, lowering his voice, he gave Paddington a knowing wink. "We instructors have to be tested every now and again as well, you know. It's my turn today."

"I didn't know," said Paddington with interest. "Perhaps I could ask you some questions on the Highway Code. I've been testing the others at breakfast all this week."

The examiner glared at him. "No you can't!" he snorted, above the sound of martial music from the radio. He looked as if he would have liked to say a good deal more, but instead he recovered himself and opened the rear door of the car for his superior to enter.

"Colonel Bogey," said the other man briefly, nodding toward the front of the car as he settled himself in the back seat.

Paddington raised his hat politely as the examiner made his way round the front of the car and climbed into the passenger seat. "Good morning, Mr. Bogey," he said.

The man clucked impatiently. He was about to explain that his superior had only been giving the name of the tune on the radio, not an introduction, but he thought better of it. Instead, he reached forward for the switch. "I think we'll have the radio off for a start," he said severely. "I can't concentrate properly with that row on and I'm sure you can't eith . . ." He broke off and a strange look came over his face as he felt the seat. "I'm sitting on something," he cried. "Something wet and sticky!"

"Oh, dear," said Paddington, looking most upset. "I expect that's my marmalade sandwiches. I put them there for my elevenses."

"Your *marmalade sandwiches*?" repeated the man as if in a dream. "They're all over my new trousers."

"Don't worry," said Paddington. He lifted up his hat and withdrew a small package. "I've got some more. I always keep some under my hat in case of an emergency."

The examiner's face seemed to go a funny color. But before he had a chance to open his mouth the man in the back reached over and tapped him on the shoulder. "Don't you think we ought to get cracking," he said meaningly. "Time's getting on and we've a lot to get through."

The examiner took a deep breath as he gathered himself together. "I take it," he said, between his teeth, "you hold a current license?"

"A *currant* license?" It was Paddington's turn to look taken aback. He'd never heard of anyone needing a license just to eat currants before. "I don't think Mrs. Bird would let me be without one," he said, giving the man a hard stare.

The examiner wilted visibly under Paddington's gaze. "Perhaps you would like to switch the engine on?" he said hastily. "We, of the Department of Transport," he continued, in an attempt to regain his normal icy calm, "do find it easier to conduct our tests actually driving along the road."

Anxious to make amends, Paddington reached forward and pushed a nearby button with one of his paws. A grinding noise came from somewhere outside.

The man in the back seat gave a cough. "I think you'll find that's the windscreen wiper, Mr. Brown," he said. "Why don't you try the button next to it?

"Don't worry," he continued, raising his voice as Paddington did as he was bidden and the engine suddenly roared into life, "we all get a little nervous at times like these."

"Oh, I'm not nervous," said Paddington. "It's just that they all look the same without my opera glasses."

"Er, quite!" The examiner gave a high-pitched laugh as he tried to humor his superior by joining in the spirit of things. "Perhaps," he said, "before we actually set out we could have a few questions on the Highway Code. Especially," he added meaningly, "as you say you've made such a study of it. What, for instance, do we look out for when we're driving at this time of the year?"

Paddington put on his thoughtful expression. "Strawberries?" he suggested, licking his lips.

"Strawberries?" repeated the examiner. "What do you mean—*strawberries*?"

"We often stop for strawberries at this time of the year," said Paddington firmly. "Mrs. Bird makes some special cream to go with them."

"I would hardly call strawberries a hazard," said the examiner petulantly.

"They are if you eat them going along," said Paddington firmly. "It's a job to know what to do with the stalks—especially if the ashtray's full."

"Good point," said the man in the back approvingly. "I must remember that one. So ought you," he added pointedly, addressing Paddington's companion.

The examiner took a deep breath. "I was thinking," he said slowly and carefully, "of sudden showers. If the weather has been dry for any length of time a sudden shower can make the road surface very slippery."

Removing a sheet of paper covered with drawings from his clipboard, he decided to have another try. "If you were going along the highway," he said, pointing to one of the drawings, "and you saw this sign, what would it mean?"

Paddington peered at the drawing. "It looks like someone trying to open an umbrella," he replied.

The examiner drew in his breath sharply. "That sign," he said, "happens to mean there are roadworks ahead."

"Perhaps they're expecting one of your showers?" suggested Paddington helpfully. He gave the man another stare. For an examiner he didn't seem to know very much.

The man returned his gaze as if in a dream. In fact, if looks could have killed, the expression on his face suggested that Paddington's name would have been added to the list of road casualties with very little bother indeed. However, once again he was saved by an impatient movement from the back of the car.

"Perhaps we should move off now?" said a voice. "We seem to be getting nowhere very fast."

"Very good," Taking a firm grip of himself, the examiner settled back in his seat. "Go straight up this road about two hundred yards," he commanded, "then when you see a sign marked BEAR LEFT . . ."

"A *bear's been left*?" Paddington suddenly sat bolt upright. He wasn't at all sure what was going on and he'd been trying to decide whether to obey his next set of instructions or wait for Mr. Brown to arrive back. The latest piece of information caused him to make up his mind very quickly indeed.

"I'm afraid I shall have to stand up to drive," he announced, as he clambered to his feet. "I can't see out properly if I'm sitting down, but I'll get there as quickly as I can."

"Now, look here," cried the examiner, a note of panic in his voice. "I didn't mean there was a *real* bear lying in the road. I only meant you're supposed to . . ." He broke off and stared at Paddington with disbelieving eyes. "What are you doing now?" he gasped, as Paddington bent down and disappeared beneath the dashboard.

"I'm putting the car into gear," gasped Paddington, as he took hold of the lever firmly with both paws. "I'm afraid it's a bit difficult with paws."

"But you can't change gear with your head under the dashboard," shrieked the examiner. "No one does that."

"Bears do," said Paddington firmly. And he gave the lever another hard tug just to show what he meant.

"Don't do it!" shouted the examiner. "Don't do it!"

"Let the clutch out!" came a voice from the back seat. "Let the clutch out!"

But if either of the men expected his cry to have any effect he was doomed to disappointment. Once Paddington got an idea firmly fixed in his mind it was very difficult to get him to change course, let alone gear, and apart from hurriedly opening the car door to let out the clutch he concentrated all his energies on the task in hand.

In the past he had often watched Mr. Brown change gear. It was something Mr. Brown prided himself on being able to do very smoothly indeed, so that really it was quite hard to know when it had actually taken place. But if Paddington hoped to emulate his example he failed miserably. As he gave the lever one final, desperate shove there was a loud grinding noise followed almost immediately by an enormous jerk as the car leaped into the air like a frustrated stallion. The force of the movement caused Paddington to fall over on his back and, in his excitement, he grabbed hold of the nearest thing to hand.

"Look out!" shrieked the examiner.

But he was too late. As Paddington tightened his grip on the accelerator pedal the car shot forward with a roar like an express train. For a second or two it seemed to hover in mid-air, and then, with a crash which made the silence that followed all the more ominous, it came to a halt again.

Paddington clambered unsteadily to his feet and peered out through the windscreen. "Oh, dear," he said, gazing round at the others. "I think we've hit a car in front."

The examiner closed his eyes. His lips were moving as if he was offering up a silent prayer.

"No," he said, slowly and distinctly. "You haven't got

it quite right. *We* haven't hit anything, *you* have. And it isn't just *a* car, it's . . ."

The examiner broke off and gazed up at the driving mirror in mute despair as his eyes caught the reflection of those belonging to his superior in the back seat.

"It happens to be mine," said a grim voice from behind.

Paddington sank back into his seat as the full horror of the situation came home to him.

"Oh, dear, Mr. Bogey," he said unhappily. "I do hope that doesn't mean you've failed your test!"

*

As with Mr. Brown's encounter with the Police, Paddington's disaster at the Test Center was a topic of conversation in the Brown household for many days afterward. Opinions as to the possible outcome were sharply divided. There were those who thought he would be bound to hear something more, and others who thought the whole thing was so complicated nothing would be done about it, but none of them quite foresaw what would happen.

One evening, just as they were sitting down to their evening meal, there was an unexpected ring at the front-door bell. Mrs. Bird hurried off to answer it, and when she returned she was accompanied, to everyone's surprise, by Paddington's examiner.

"Please don't get up," he exclaimed, as Paddington jumped to his feet in alarm and hurried round to the far side of the table for safety.

He removed a large brown envelope from his briefcase and placed it on the table in front of Paddington's plate. "I . . . er . . . I happened to be passing so I thought I would drop this in for young Mr. Brown."

"Oh, dear," said Mrs. Brown nervously. "It looks very official. I do hope it isn't bad news."

The man permitted himself a smile. "Nothing like that," he said. "Congratulations on passing your test," he continued, turning to Mr. Brown. "I was glad to hear you were able to take it again so quickly. All's well that ends well, and I'm sure you'll be pleased to know that now my superior officer has had his bumper straightened you'd hardly know anything had happened."

He mopped his brow with a handkerchief as the memory of it came flooding back. "It all sounded much worse than it actually was. As you know, I was being examined myself at the time, so I was under a certain amount of strain. As a matter of fact, I came through with flying colors. The chief examiner thought that in the circumstances I did extremely well. He's even recommended me for promotion."

"But whatever is it?" cried Judy, as Paddington opened the envelope and withdrew a sheet of paper with an inscription on it.

The examiner gave a cough. "It's a special test certificate," he said. "It enables the owner to drive vehicles in group S."

"Trust Paddington!" said Jonathan. "I bet he's the only one who's ever driven into the back of an examiner's car *and* still passed his test into the bargain."

Mr. Brown gave the examiner a puzzled look. "Group *S*?" he repeated. "I didn't know there was such a thing."

"It's very rare." The examiner permitted himself another smile. "In fact there probably isn't another one like it in the whole world. It's for shopping baskets on wheels. I noticed young Mr. Brown had one with him at the time of our . . . er . . . meeting."

"Gosh, Paddington," Judy gazed at him in relief. "What are you going to do with it?"

Paddington considered the matter for a moment. He really felt quite overwhelmed by his latest piece of good fortune. "I think," he announced at last, "I shall fix it to the front of my basket. Then if I ever have trouble at the supermarket cash desk I shall be able to show it."

"What a good idea," said the examiner, looking very pleased at the reception his gift had met. "And you'll be pleased to see it's made out for life. That means," he added, gently but firmly, "that you need never, ever, *ever* come and see us to take your test again!"

CHAPTER TWO

In and Out of Trouble

ONE MORNING, soon after the visit from the driving examiner, Paddington was pottering about in the garden doing some testing of his own in order to make sure Mr. Brown's fruit was properly ripe, when he happened to glance through a knothole in the nearby fence. As he did so he nearly fell over backwards into the raspberry canes with astonishment at the sight which met his eyes.

The fence belonged to the Browns' neighbor, Mr. Curry, and in the normal course of events there was seldom anything of any great interest to see. Gardening wasn't one of Mr. Curry's strong points. Apart from one or two shrubs and a couple of old trees, most of the ground was given over to what he called "the lawn," but which in reality was nothing more than a patch of rough grass.

For once, however, it was looking unusually neat and tidy. In fact, overnight it had undergone nothing less than a transformation. The grass had been newly mown, the bushes pruned, and the trees had been lopped of their lower branches. There was even a small table in the center of the lawn on which had been placed a tray with a glass and a jug of what looked like orangeade.

Paddington rubbed his eyes and then took a closer look through the hole. Now that he thought about it, he remembered hearing the sound of sawing the day before. At the time he hadn't taken much notice of it, and never in his wildest dreams had he pictured it coming from Mr. Curry's garden.

The Browns' neighbor had obviously been busy, but it wasn't the view of his actual garden, nor the orangeade that caused Paddington's astonishment; it was the sight of something very odd suspended between the two trees. At first glance it seemed to be a cross between a very large hairnet that had been hung out to dry, and some overgrown knitting that had gone sadly wrong; in fact he couldn't remember having seen anything quite like it before in the whole of his life.

It was all very strange and Paddington was about to go indoors in order to tell Mrs. Bird about it when he had his second shock of the morning.

Having rubbed his eyes once more so as to make doubly sure he wasn't dreaming the whole thing, he opened them again in order to take one last look, only to find to his surprise that the scene had disappeared. Something or other was now covering up the knothole.

Paddington was not the sort of bear to be beaten by such trifles. After finding a suitable cane from among the pile in the raspberry patch, he bent down again and poked it through the hole as hard as he could in order

to remove the offending object. A second later the cane fell from his paw like a red-hot poker as a yell of pain rang round the garden.

"Bear!" roared a familiar voice. "Is that you, bear? How dare you!"

Paddington scrambled to his feet and gazed mournfully at the sight of the Browns' neighbor as he bobbed up and down on one leg on the other side of the fence.

"That was my shin you poked, bear!" howled Mr. Curry. "What were you doing? Spying on me? Mark my words . . . I shall report you for this!"

"Oh, no, Mr. Curry," gasped Paddington. "I wasn't *spying*. I wouldn't do that. I was only trying to see what was going on. There's something hanging from your trees and I wondered if you knew about it."

"What's that, bear?" Mr. Curry hopped closer to the fence and gave a snort as he peered over the top. "Of course I know about it. I put it there. There's no need to go around telling everyone."

"Oh, I wasn't going to tell *everyone*, Mr. Curry," said Paddington earnestly. "Only Mrs. Bird."

"Mrs. Bird!" For some reason best known to himself, Paddington's words had a strange effect on Mr. Curry. He stopped rubbing his leg and drew nearer the fence. "Come now, bear," he said. "There's no need to do that. It's only a hammock. Haven't you ever seen one before?"

"A hammock, Mr. Curry?" repeated Paddington. "No, I don't think I have."

"Hmm." Mr. Curry looked somewhat relieved by Paddington's reply. "Well, bear," he said, in a slightly better humor, "a hammock is what sailors used to sleep in on board ship. Nowadays they have bunks, but people still use hammocks in their gardens. They're ideal for relaxing in. There's nothing nicer on a warm summer afternoon than a quiet doze in a hammock. Provided," he added meaningly, "there are no unseemly interruptions from the neighbors!"

Paddington looked most surprised as he listened to all Mr. Curry had to say on the subject of hammocks. "I've never heard of a bed with holes in it before," he exclaimed. "Is it safe?"

"Safe?" Mr. Curry gave another snort. "*Safe?* Of course it's safe! Why shouldn't it be? What's wrong with it?" he demanded.

"Oh, I didn't mean yours wasn't a *good* one, Mr. Curry," said Paddington hastily, anxious to make amends. "It's just that it looks rather old . . . I mean . . . have you had it very long?" he added lamely.

"Er . . . well, I . . ." Mr. Curry broke into a loud cough. Once again he seemed anxious to change the subject. He glanced around to make sure no one else was about and then stared thoughtfully at Paddington.

"How much do you weigh, bear?"he barked.

Paddington was taken by surprise at the question. The Browns' neighbor had a habit of turning matters to his own ends and it was sometimes difficult to follow what he had in mind. "I don't know, Mr. Curry," he said, cautiously playing for time. "Sometimes I weigh a lot—sometimes I don't. It depends on how many marmalade sandwiches I've eaten. Mrs. Bird says it must be over a ton sometimes after Sunday lunch."

"Hmm." Mr. Curry considered Paddington's answer for a moment and then came to a decision. "Look, bear," he said, as he removed a piece of the fence in order to make room for Paddington to climb through, "you can do me a little favor if you like. I'm just going upstairs to change. I shall only be five minutes, but while I'm gone you can test my hammock for me as a treat . . . just to make sure it's sa . . . er . . . *comfortable*.

"But make sure you do it properly," he continued, as he helped Paddington through the gap in the fence. "And no helping yourself to my orangeade while I'm not looking. I've marked the jug, so I shall know at once."

Mr. Curry broke off and took a closer look at Paddington's whiskers, several of which had some suspiciously red stains on them. "While you're at it," he said, "you might like to gather a few raspberries for me. If you do I *may* let you have a proper go with the hammock later on . . . *after* I've finished with it for the day."

"Thank you very much, Mr. Curry," said Paddington doubtfully. "I shall look forward to that."

He gazed unhappily after the retreating figure of the Browns' neighbor. Doing favors for Mr. Curry was something which had long ago lost its appeal; more often than not things went wrong. For a moment or two he toyed with the idea of climbing back through the fence and going to see Mrs. Bird first, but he hastily changed his mind as Mr. Curry turned and gave him a final glare before disappearing down the side of his house.

Pushing his doubts to one side, Paddington turned his attention to the hammock. He was the sort of bear who liked anything new, or, at least, anything which was new to him; for seen at close quarters, the hammock looked, if possible, even older than it had from a distance.

Although, as Mr. Curry had explained to him, the hammock was meant to have holes, some of them looked far larger than they had started off as originally, and all in all Paddington decided he didn't much like the look of it.

But it was when he actually tried to climb into it that his troubles really began, for he soon discovered that looking at a hammock is one thing; getting into one is quite another matter.

To start with, it was rather higher off the ground than he would have liked, and not for the first time Paddington found himself wishing bears were born with longer legs, for when he tried to lift one of his up in order to climb in, it didn't come anywhere near the edge.

Trying a different approach, Paddington grasped the hammock from underneath with both paws, then taking a deep breath he heaved both legs off the ground in the hope of getting them round the middle and gripping it from either side like a pair of pincers.

The first part of his maneuver went very well indeed, and for several moments he hung suspended beneath the hammock while he took stock of the situation. It was when he tried to carry out his next move that things started to go wrong, for without Wellington boots his claws got stuck in the rope mesh and try as he might he couldn't free them. In the end he had to let go with his paws and hope for the best. For a moment or two he hung upside down with his head a few inches from the ground until there was a sudden "ping" and the string broke.

Paddington felt very glad he'd been wearing his hat, for Mr. Curry's lawn felt decidedly hard. As it was, the marmalade sandwich he usually kept there in case of an emergency went some way toward breaking his fall, and for a moment or two he lay where he was gasping for breath while he tried hard to think of some other way of tackling the problem.

Without a book of instructions it was very hard, and in the end he decided the only answer was to take the bull by the horns and make a run at it. Crossing to the far side of the lawn he took another deep breath, pulled his hat down over his ears, and then hurried toward the hammock as fast as his legs would carry him. As it

loomed up in front of him he took a tremendous leap in the air, and clutched blindly at the first thing which met his grasp.

Paddington wasn't quite sure what happened next. He was vaguely aware of a feeling of relief as his paws met with rope, which he clung to as hard as he could, then to his relief he felt the rest of him land in something soft. After that everything became a blur. Almost at once he started spinning round and round like a top. Gradually, however, the spinning slowed down until at last he came to a stop with only his head poking out. The rest of him had the appearance of a tightly trussed chicken; one moreover which was not only oven-ready but practically ready to serve up for Sunday lunch. Far from being relaxed in the way Mr. Curry had described, Paddington felt more like a sailor who had just rounded Cape Horn during a particularly bad storm.

But the worst was yet to come. He hardly had time to free one of his paws in order to make sure his hat was still on when he felt himself start to spin in the opposite direction, slowly at first, then with ever-increasing speed, until he was suddenly ejected from the hammock like a stone from a catapult, only to land on the ground a moment later in almost the very same spot as before.

This time he lay where he was for rather longer, while he considered his next move. Paddington wasn't the sort of bear to be beaten by trifles. In fact, the more things went wrong the more determined he usually became to put them to rights.

It was as he lay gazing up at the sky while he pondered the matter that he suddenly caught sight of something dangling overhead, and as he did so another idea gradually entered his mind.

In his haste to clear a space so that he could erect the hammock between the two trees, Mr. Curry had left a rope tied to one of the upper branches.

Paddington came to a decision. Mr. Curry's fruit trees were old and rather gnarled and just right for climbing. Having made up his mind, in no time at all Paddington was up one of the trunks and sitting astride a main branch ready for action. Grasping it firmly with his legs he reached over to grip the rope and then began lowering himself gently down it to a point where he was directly over the middle of the hammock.

Feeling very pleased with himself, Paddington paused for a moment in order to mop his brow before continuing. As he did so he noticed a particularly juicy-looking apple only a few inches away. He licked his lips. Climbing trees was hard work and he felt sure that even Mr. Curry wouldn't begrudge one small apple from so many in the circumstances.

Hastily stuffing the handkerchief back into his duffle

coat pocket he reached out his paw and was about to remove it from the branch when an upstairs window in Mr. Curry's house suddenly shot open and the familiar face of the Browns' neighbor appeared. As he caught sight of Paddington his eyes nearly popped out of their sockets and his face started to go a funny color.

"Bear!" he bellowed. "What are you doing now, bear? How dare you pick my apples without permission. Get down off that rope at once!"

"Oh, dear, Mr. Curry," gasped Paddington. "I wasn't *climbing* your rope—I was coming down. I . . ." In his confusion Paddington tried to let go of the apple with one paw and raise his hat with the other. A moment later, and for what seemed like the umpteenth time that morning, he felt himself falling through space.

Paddington closed his eyes tightly and braced himself for the shock, but in the event it came rather later than he expected. The delay was only for a fraction of a second, but it was accompanied by a very ominous rending sound indeed, one moreover which caused Mr. Curry's face to go an even deeper shade of purple than it had been before. If the Browns' neighbor had found it hard to believe his eyes when he'd first seen Paddington up his tree, he found it even more difficult as he gazed at the gaping hole in the middle of his hammock through which Paddington had just passed. For once he seemed totally at a loss for words.

"Bear!" he spluttered at long last. "Bear! What have you done to my hammock? Come back at once, bear!"

But Paddington had disappeared. Without even bothering to look back he dived through the hole in the fence as if his very life depended on it. He'd had quite enough of hammocks for one day—especially ones which belonged to Mr. Curry.

*

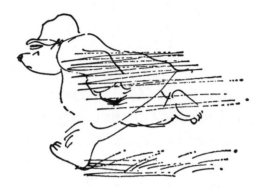

Mrs. Bird gave a snort as she listened to Paddington's tale of woe later that same day. "*His* hammock, indeed!" she exclaimed. "The cheek of it. That's *our* old hammock. Mr. Brown came across it when he was clearing out the garage the other day."

"It's been in there for years," agreed Mrs. Brown. "No wonder you went straight through it. It was as rotten as they come."

"Mr. Curry ought to think himself lucky he didn't go through it," said Judy. "I bet we should never have heard the last of it if he had."

"Dad put it out for the dustmen yesterday morning," explained Jonathan. "Mr. Curry must have seen it and taken it away before they arrived. The old scrounger."

Paddington listened to the conversation with growing surprise. Although he'd often been in Mr. Brown's garage he'd never come across the hammock before; not that he would have known what it was if he had found it. Now he rather wished he'd been able to have a proper go when it was all right to use.

"Perhaps," he said hopefully, "I could sew some holes together and make you a new one. Bears are quite good at that sort of thing."

The Browns exchanged glances. "Shall we tell him?" asked Jonathan.

Judy glanced out of the window. "Let's," she said. "I think Daddy's almost ready." And without further ado she led the way into the garden.

Paddington looked more and more mystified as he followed on behind.

"There!" said Judy when they were all outside. And she pointed toward the middle of the lawn.

Paddington nearly fell over backwards with surprise again as he received his third shock of the morning. For there, in the middle of the grass, was another hammock, suspended between two poles of a large frame.

"It's a special stand," explained Jonathan. "That means it'll be easier to climb into . . ."

"And *much* safer once you're in," added Judy.

Mr. Brown stood back in order to admire the result of his labors, then he turned to Paddington. "If you like," he said generously, "you can be the first to test it."

Paddington considered the matter carefully for a moment or two as he approached the hammock and took a closer look at it. Then he stood back and held out his paw.

"No, thank you, Mr. Brown," he announced politely. "After you!

"In fact," he added hastily, in case the others insisted, "After *everyone*!"

CHAPTER THREE

Paddington and the Stately Home

PADDINGTON'S FRIEND MR. GRUBER chuckled no end when he heard about the goings-on with Mr. Curry's hammock.

"There's many a slip 'twixt cup and lip, Mr. Brown," he said. "Or in this case 'twixt the hammock and the ground. I think I shall stick to my old horse-hair sofa."

Paddington nodded his agreement from behind a cloud of cocoa steam. It was good to be back in the comparative safety of Mr. Gruber's antique shop, enjoying a chat over their morning elevenses.

"Mind you," continued Mr. Gruber, as Paddington handed him a bun from his morning supply, "I must say all this talk of hammocks takes me back to the days when I was a boy. Many a happy hour I spent in the garden during the school holidays, munching an apple and reading a book as I swung to and fro in the sunshine." Mr. Gruber gave a sigh and a dreamy expression came over his face as he cast his mind back. "It's probably only my imagination, Mr. Brown, but the summers always seemed longer and warmer in those days—especially in my native Hungary."

Paddington nearly fell off the sofa with surprise at Mr. Gruber's words. As long as he'd known him his friend had always seemed the same—neither young nor old, and it was hard to picture him looking any different.

Mr. Gruber chuckled again as he caught sight of the expression on Paddington's face.

"All that was many moons ago, Mr. Brown." He waved his hand in a circular motion over his head to take in the contents of the shop. "In those days lots of the things you see around you here were ordinary everyday objects such as you or I would use—or throw out when we'd finished with them. Now, people pay ten or even a hundred times what they cost in the first place."

Paddington took another bite out of his bun and then gazed around Mr. Gruber's shop. He was so used to the scene he rather took for granted all the various items of gold and silver and copper and bronze; the pictures, and the piles of bric-a-brac which sometimes filled it full almost to overflowing. The thought that once upon a time people had actually used some of Mr. Gruber's antiques had never really occurred to him before and it made him see everything in a new light.

"Times change," said Mr. Gruber sadly, "sometimes for the better and sometimes for the not so good. Nowadays the only time you see many of these things is in an antique shop like mine or in a Stately Home."

"A Stately Home, Mr. Gruber?" exclaimed Paddington. "I don't think I've ever been in one of those."

It was Mr. Gruber's turn to look surprised. "You've never been inside a Stately Home, Mr. Brown?" he repeated. *"Never?"*

Paddington considered the matter for a moment while Mr. Gruber topped up his cocoa. "I've been to the Home for Retired Bears in Lima," he said at last. "The one where Aunt Lucy lives. But I don't think that was very stately."

Mr. Gruber slapped his knee. "In that case, Mr. Brown," he said, "I have an idea. Tomorrow is early closing; it's about time we had one of our little outings and I've been racking my brains trying to think where to take you. Tomorrow," he said impressively, "tomorrow, Mr. Brown, I will take you to a Stately Home!"

Paddington could hardly believe his ears and he grew more and more excited as he hurried home in order to tell the others.

Mr. Gruber had also invited Jonathan and Judy along to share the outing and they, too, could hardly wait when he told them the good news.

That night Paddington had an extra-special bath in honor of the occasion and at Mrs. Bird's suggestion he went to bed early so that he would be fully rested the next day.

"I think Paddington ought to go on more outings," said Mrs. Brown, as he disappeared up the stairs. "I've never seen him quite so spick and span. He looks like a new bear."

"Hmm," said the Browns' housekeeper. "That's as may be, but beauty's only fur deep. It's still the same underneath and I'd sooner Mr. Gruber than me. Any home that bear visits is likely to be in a state rather than stately by the time he's finished with it."

Mrs. Bird spoke from bitter experience of past outings. Nevertheless, when Mr. Gruber turned up the next day and set off down the road with his party even she had to admit that Paddington's appearance would have raised the tone of any expedition.

His duffle coat had been freshly ironed; his hat newly washed; and even his Wellington boots had an extra-special shine to them.

Mr. Gruber had come armed with a plentiful supply of books and maps to while away their journey, and as they changed from bus to train and then back to a bus again he told them about Stately Homes in general and the one he was taking them to in particular.

"The problem is," he explained, as they neared their destination, "no one can really afford to run a Stately Home any longer, so the owners have to open them up to the public, and to make the public want to come they have to offer other things besides. Some have Safari Parks, where they have lots of lions and tigers; others have Fun Fairs. The one we're going to is Luckham House where they specialize in concerts. It has a very good restaurant into the bargain as well. Lord Luckham likes his food."

Mr. Gruber smiled as they alighted from the bus outside some large wrought-iron gates and he caught sight of the expression on Paddington's face. "I thought that might appeal to you, Mr. Brown," he said. "I know how much you like music."

Judy took hold of Paddington's paw as they made their way up the long drive. "I think someone's pulling your leg," she whispered. "I happen to know Mr. Gruber's treating us all to dinner tonight."

Paddington licked his lips. He always enjoyed eating out and to have a meal in a Stately Home sounded very good value indeed.

"They do a very good Beef Wellington," said Mr. Gruber, as he caught the tail end of the conversation. "It's one of Lord Luckham's specialities. I had one the last time I was here and I'm looking forward to repeating the experience."

Paddington had never heard of Beef Wellington before, but apart from explaining that it was beef cooked in a special kind of casing, Mr. Gruber refused to be drawn on the subject. "A surprise is not a surprise if you know all about it, Mr. Brown," he said, and he directed their attention to some of the other delights they had in store.

As it happened there were so many things to see, Paddington soon forgot about his forthcoming meal anyway. It was really like strolling through another world; a giant version of Mr. Gruber's shop and the rest of the Portobello Market rolled into one, with everything from collections of china and dolls to a giant four-poster bed, in which, according to Mr. Gruber's

notes, Queen Elizabeth the First had once slept while on her way to York.

Paddington was most impressed. All the same, what with walking through endless galleries lined with pictures, not to mention climbing innumerable flights of stairs—more of which seemed to go up than ever came down again—he was more than glad when at long last Mr. Gruber ushered them into a large chair-filled room where the concert was due to take place.

Paddington had never been to a concert before and he applauded loudly as a man in a dark suit climbed on to the platform and crossed to a piano.

Mr. Gruber gave a cough. "I rather think," he whispered, "he's only come to open the piano lid." But like the kindly man he was, he joined in Paddington's applause in order to save his friend embarrassment.

Fortunately Paddington was able to continue his applause as almost at once a second man approached the front of the stage and began announcing the first item on the program; a selection of songs from famous operas rendered by a Miss Olive Marks and a Mr. Gilbert Street, who were billed as "Partners in Song." Following Mr. Gruber's example, he cupped his chin in

his paws and then sat forward eagerly in his seat, ready to take it all in.

Gradually, however, his smile became more and more fixed and he gazed anxiously up at the ceiling as Miss Marks opened her mouth and first one piercing note then another emerged and began rattling the chandeliers overhead. He rather wished he'd put his ears instead of his chin inside his paws, but it was much too late to change his mind.

Miss Marks was nothing if not generous with her notes, although from the look on her face and the way she rolled her eyes, the effort obviously caused her a certain amount of pain; a pain that was certainly being shared by a high percentage of her audience. In fact it was noticeable that even her partner, Mr. Street, was careful to stand well clear.

That apart, as far as Paddington could make out it seemed to take her twice as long as anyone he'd ever met before to make up her mind about even the simplest thing. Three times she announced in song that she would like to close the window, and as many times again that she was about to leave. However, ten minutes later, when Gilbert Street knelt at her feet in order to sing, the window was still wide open and Miss Marks very much on stage.

Mr. Street had chosen an aria called "Your Tiny

Hand Is Frozen," but there was nothing in the least bit small about any part of the object of his affections, let alone her hand. Far from being tiny, Miss Marks's hand was one of the largest Paddington had ever seen, and under the heat of the overhead lights it glistened like a freshly boiled lobster.

Paddington's applause as the couple finally took their leave was louder than most, and caused Mr. Gruber to cast an anxious glance in his direction.

"I shouldn't clap too loudly, Mr. Brown," he whispered in an aside. "They might do an encore."

In his haste to stop clapping Paddington dropped his program on the floor and, captured by a draught from a nearby door, it sailed several rows away.

"Oh, dear!" Judy caught her brother's eye and gave a groan as Paddington disappeared from view and began peering between the legs of the people in front.

But luckily for her own and her brother's peace of mind, the disturbance was covered by the arrival on stage of a group of musicians who were due to play some works by Mozart.

During Paddington's temporary absence, and while the music stands were being arranged, Mr. Gruber passed the time by explaining the next item to Jonathan and Judy.

"If you look on your program," he said, "you will see

it's got a number after it . . . K280. That's the cata-
logue number to make sure the works were always
played in the right order. In German it's called a Köchel
number, after the man who catalogued Mozart's
works."

"What's that, Mr. Gruber?" called Paddington, as he
climbed into view again. "We're going to have some
cocoa?" He licked his lips in anticipation at the
thought. Crawling about on the floor looking for a program was thirsty work—especially in a duffle coat.

"Not cocoa . . . Köchel . . ." began Judy. "That's
quite a different matter." She gave another sigh. It was
sometimes rather difficult explaining matters to
Paddington.

"Köchel?" repeated Paddington in surprise. "I don't
think I've ever tasted any of that before."

"Ssh!" said someone loudly from behind as the first
notes of music filled the air.

Paddington turned and gave the person who'd
shushed a hard stare before directing his attention to
the platform. He couldn't see any mugs let alone cups
and saucers, and during a particularly loud passage of
music he consulted the program once again. It was a bit
hard to see as the lights in the audience had been
dimmed. Apart from that there were one or two foot-
marks where it had been trodden on, which made it

even more difficult to read, but for the life of him he couldn't see any mention of refreshments being served.

It was as he began reading about the item being played that his face fell still further. According to the notes there were fifteen variations to be got through. Paddington didn't think much of the original version let alone any possible variations. He was quite keen on music, but his tastes ran more toward the loud kind which could be rendered on a comb and paper rather than the complicated variety.

He stole a sidelong glance at Mr. Gruber, but his friend had his eyes closed in order to concentrate on the music, and beyond him Jonathan and Judy appeared to be making a close study of the chandeliers.

Paddington came to a decision. He had no wish to offend his friend, especially as he had gone to so much trouble, but from the look of rapture on Mr. Gruber's face there was little fear of that.

A few moments later, taking advantage of another loud passage, he made a move, only this time it was in the direction of a door marked EXIT.

It had been a long and tiring afternoon and Paddington knew just the very spot where he wanted most of all to be at that very moment. It was up some stairs at the end of a long corridor and it was labeled QUEEN ELIZABETH'S ROOM.

Having a bed with curtains round it seemed a very good idea indeed—especially if you didn't want to be disturbed.

In much less time than it would have taken Miss Marks to sing Jack Robinson, Paddington was up the stairs, into the room, and pulling the curtains tightly round him. They came together with a satisfying swish and with a sigh of contentment he closed his eyes and lay back with his head on the pillow, drinking in the sound of distant music and the faint aroma of something delicious as it wafted up from the nearby kitchens.

But Paddington's satisfaction was short-lived. In the normal course of events he was quite good at sleeping; given a few cushions or an armchair by the fire he could be away in no time at all. But gradually it dawned on him that he had never been less comfortable in his life. Compared with his own bed at Windsor Gardens it was like trying to sleep on boards; boards moreover which contained more than their fair share of knots, and he could quite see why Queen Elizabeth the First had only stayed one night.

He tried lying on top of the pillow, but if anything it was even more lumpy than the bed. The bird used to provide the stuffing had obviously suffered from a bad attack of hardening of the feathers, for the ends stuck out through their outer covering like thorns on a rose bush.

Paddington's opinion of life in a Stately Home reached a new low, and he was about to try his luck elsewhere when he heard voices and the door to the room suddenly opened.

Closing his eyes again as tightly as they would go, Paddington lay where he was, hardly daring to breathe. He was only just in time, for a split second later the curtains round the bed were flung open and whoever had been talking broke off in mid-sentence.

"Blimey!" said a voice. "Is that 'er?"

"That's what it says in the guide," came a woman's voice. "Queen Elizabeth slept 'ere on the way to York."

"Who'd 'ave thought it," came the first voice again. "No wonder she never got married." The owner of the voice gave a sniff. "Smells of marmalade too. Enough to put anyone off. 'Course, they never went in for washing much in them days."

"Didn't know they wore duffle coats either," added his friend. "The things you learn. Only goes to show."

If stares had been made capable of passing through closed eyelids, the two speakers would have received the full benefit of one of Paddington's hardest ever. As it was, blissfully unaware of their narrow escape, they pulled the curtains together and continued their tour of the room.

Left on his own again, Paddington was about to relax when all that had been said before was suddenly wiped from his mind as he caught another snatch of conversation.

"Pity about the Beef Wellington being off," said the man. "Sounded a bit of all right, that."

"I know," said his companion sympathetically, "'ad me taste buds all of a-quiver it did. The waiter said they was 'aving trouble with the pastry chef and . . ."

Paddington strained his ears in an effort to catch the

rest of the conversation, but it was cut off in mid-air by a click as the door swung shut and the speakers continued on their way.

For a moment he lay where he was, growing more and more upset. It wasn't often Mr. Gruber gave himself a treat, and when he did he always made sure he shared it with others. One of the things he'd specially mentioned about the present outing was the Beef Wellington, and the thought of his being done out of it was most upsetting. Paddington had a strong sense of right and wrong. When he finally sat up the look on his face was not dissimilar to the one the previous occupant of the bed, Queen Elizabeth the First, must have worn the day she ordered Sir Francis Drake to do battle with the Spanish Fleet. It was a look which Paddington kept reserved for very special occasions and it boded ill for anyone who got in his way before his plans were complete.

Carefully removing his boots, he picked them up in his paw, tiptoed across the room, opened the door, peered out in order to make sure the coast was clear, and then hurried off down the corridor in the direction of the kitchen as fast as his legs would carry him.

*

Mr. Gruber picked up his knife and fork and gazed reflectively across the dining-table as he prepared to do justice to his meal.

There was something distinctly odd about the way Paddington was behaving. It wasn't just the guilty expression on his face, or the fact that he'd arrived back in the concert hall only seconds before the end of the program; the two might well have gone together. It wasn't even the patches of white stuff—rather like flour—all over his duffle coat. It was almost as if something was missing, but for the life of him he couldn't think what it could be.

Then there was the question of the meal. Mr. Gruber would have bet anything that Paddington would have chosen the same as everyone else, but in the event he'd stuck out very firmly for steak and kidney pie.

"Aren't you going to make a start, Mr. Brown?" he asked. "You don't want to let it get cold."

"I'd really like to see how you get on first, Mr. Gruber," said Paddington politely.

Mr. Gruber hesitated. After making so much of the Beef Wellington he felt rather bad about complaining, but it really was giving off a very strange odor. Rubbery almost. Also, although the knife looked extremely sharp, he was finding it difficult if not impossible to cut beyond the pastry covering.

Jonathan and Judy exchanged glances. The same thought was passing through both their minds, but before they had a chance to say anything there was a commotion at a nearby table as a man threw down his cutlery and jumped to his feet.

"I demand to see Lord Luckham!" he exclaimed. "This meat is as tough as old boots. I've never tasted anything like it."

"*Old* boots!" exclaimed Paddington hotly, as he jumped to his feet. "They're not old. They're my best Wellingtons. I wore them specially for the occasion and I only cleaned them last night."

Jonathan took a quick look down at Paddington's feet and as he did so his jaw dropped. "Crikey!" he groaned, as a tall distinguished-looking man hurried across the Great Hall toward them. "Here we go again!"

If it took the combined efforts of Mr. Gruber, Jonathan, and Judy some while to explain to Lord Luckham and the other diners the whys and wherefores of how Paddington's Wellington boots came to be inside their pastry, it took them even longer to explain to Paddington why they shouldn't have been there in the first place. He looked most aggrieved about the whole idea of calling something by the wrong name. It was very confusing.

In the end it was Lord Luckham himself who came to the rescue. He announced that not only would anything else his guests like to order be "on the house" that evening, but that he would be inviting all those present to a special Gala evening just as soon as it could be arranged.

"I shall personally supervise the making of our famous Beef Wellington," he boomed, amid general applause, "and I shall serve it with some of my own Béarnaise sauce into the bargain."

"To tell you the truth," he said later that evening, when Mr. Gruber thanked him for his generous action, "I happen to know there's a certain person from a well-known newspaper here tonight, and I don't doubt we shall be reading all about it in tomorrow's editions.

"We at Luckham House can always do with publicity," he added, as he shook Paddington by the paw. "If you have any other ideas we shall be pleased to hear about them. I'm sure you'll agree it will be a very sad day if we ever have to give up what we are doing."

Paddington joined in the general agreement at this last

remark. One way and another, despite all that had gone wrong, he'd enjoyed his visit to a Stately Home. Now he was looking forward to going back to the comfort of his own bed at number thirty-two Windsor Gardens.

"It was very kind of Lord Luckham to invite us back," said Judy, as they waved goodbye and made their way back down the long drive.

"Very kind," agreed Mr. Gruber. "You'll be able to see what a real Beef Wellington tastes like, Mr. Brown. Will you like that?"

Paddington considered the matter for a moment. "I think so, Mr. Gruber," he announced at last. "But if you don't mind I won't have any 'Bears-nose' sauce with mine. I don't think that sounds very nice at all."

CHAPTER FOUR

Paddington and "Bob-a-Job"

MRS. BROWN PAUSED at her washing for a moment and then heaved a deep sigh as she glanced out of the kitchen window. "I wonder who thought up the idea for 'bob-a-job' week in the first place?" she said.

Mrs. Bird gave a snort as she joined Mrs. Brown at the window and directed her gaze toward the bottom of the garden, where a small figure in blue was struggling beneath a heavily laden clothes line. "Whoever it was they couldn't have had bears in mind," she replied. "If they'd known Paddington was going to lend a paw they would have had second thoughts. I feel quite worn out with it all."

"It isn't that I want to discourage him," she continued, averting her eyes as something white fluttered to the ground, "but I sometimes think it would be cheaper and quicker in the long run to pay twice as much *not* to have things done."

The Browns' housekeeper spoke with feeling, for Paddington's involvement with "bob-a-job" week was a sore subject in the household.

It had all started a few days before when he'd come across an item in the local paper about the Scouts. According to the article, the local group were visiting houses in the neighborhood all that week offering their services for the sum of five pence a go. No job, it said, would be too big or too small, and at the end of the week they planned to hold a jamboree in the Town Hall in aid of charity.

Although Paddington had never actually been in the Scouts, or even the Cubs for that matter, the thought of making himself useful and being paid for it at the same time struck him as a very good idea indeed, and with the week already half over he lost no time in getting down to work.

Jonathan gave him an old tent which had been cleared out of the garage at the same time as the hammock, and Paddington had erected it on the lawn so that he could use it as his headquarters.

The article had ended by saying that after each visit the Scouts would leave a special sticker with a tick printed on it which the occupant of the house could display to show that the job had been satisfactorily completed.

It was the decision to make his own stickers that had been the start of Paddington's undoing. He wasn't the sort of bear who believed in doing things by halves, and he'd sat up in bed quite late the first night carefully

transferring his paw print from an ink pad on to some labels Mrs. Bird had given him from her jam-making outfit. But in the event he hadn't been careful enough. By the time he went to turn out the light he found to his dismay that his sheets looked as if they'd been the subject of a none-too-successful "bob-a-job" week themselves. They were covered from top to bottom with paw prints, and not for the first time Paddington wished he'd picked a less unusual mark to show that things were genuinely his, for there was no disguising who was to blame.

It was a bad start. He felt he couldn't actually charge anything for washing the sheets, even though it took the best part of a day and innumerable goes with a scrubbing brush and soap to get them clean again.

The fact that all the washing had left his paws clean for making the custard the following evening didn't go as well as he'd hoped either. Paddington liked making custard and normally he was very good at it, but for once everything seemed to go wrong. He wasn't sure if it was because he was worn out after all his hard work, or whether it simply wasn't his day, but as things turned out he made far too much and it all boiled over, landing on Mrs. Bird's clean laundry and ruining the saucepan into the bargain at the same time; all of which had taken several more hours to put right.

The truth was that despite all his hard work the front window of the Browns' house was still sadly lacking in stickers, and he hadn't a single penny, let alone any bobs, to show for it.

Even the simple act of putting the clothes out to dry seemed to have problems, for Mrs. Bird's expanding clothes line had been stretched beyond its limits and a good deal of the washing was already gathering fresh dirt as it trailed on the ground.

All in all, Paddington felt he'd done enough jobs to last a lifetime, and with dark hints from Mrs. Bird that she expected to see her washing as she'd left it, the chances of progressing beyond number thirty-two Windsor Gardens seemed very remote indeed.

The more Paddington considered the matter the more gloomy his prospects appeared to be; in fact he was so deep in thought it was some while before he realized with a start that someone was calling his name.

Emerging from behind a large sheet, he removed a pillowcase from his head only to discover to his dismay that the voice belonged to Mr. Curry.

Paddington had kept well clear of the Browns' neighbor ever since the episode with the hammock; in fact if he'd been asked to name all the people he least wanted to talk to, Mr. Curry would have been very high on the list indeed, and for a moment he toyed with the idea of putting the pillowcase over his head again, but it was too late.

However, for once the Browns' neighbor seemed in an unusually friendly mood.

"Glad to see you're busy, bear," he called, as he peered over the top of the fence. "Idle paws make for mischief—that's what I always say."

"Oh, my paws haven't been idle for a long time, Mr. Curry," said Paddington earnestly. "I'm doing 'bob-a-job' week and it's keeping me very busy."

"'Bob-a-job' week?" Mr. Curry rubbed his hands together with invisible soap. "That's a coincidence. I hope you're putting the money to a good cause. Not frittering it away."

"Oh, yes, Mr. Curry," said Paddington. "I'm sending it all to the Home for Retired Bears in Lima. That is, if I get any," he added sadly.

"Hmm." Mr. Curry cleared his throat. "Er . . . talking of 'bob-a-job' week, I was wondering if you would care to do *me* a favor, bear?" He bent down for a moment in order to undo a parcel he'd been carrying and then reappeared holding a frilly white object. "I have a dress shirt which needs seeing to. I was just going to take it to the cleaners but I need it this evening and they always charge extra if you want things back in a hurry.

I wonder if you have any spare room on your line?"

"Why, yes, Mr. Curry." Paddington looked most relieved as he hurried forward to take the shirt. "I'd be very pleased."

"Now, take care of it, bear!" barked Mr. Curry, some of his more normal bad-temper coming to the fore. "It's a very expensive shirt and it's meant for special occasions. No dropping it in the mud, mind."

The Browns' neighbor looked around carefully and then lowered his voice. "As a matter of fact I'm going to the jamboree tonight. There's a fancy-dress parade and I'm going as Beau Brummell, the famous dandy."

Paddington's eyes grew larger and larger as he listened to Mr. Curry. He'd never pictured the Browns' neighbor joining in any sort of parade, let alone a fancy-dress one as a Brummell.

"I hope your bows stay in place, Mr. Curry," he exclaimed as he eyed the shirt.

Mr. Curry glared at him suspiciously. "Are you making fun of me, bear?" he barked.

"Oh, no, Mr. Curry," said Paddington, "there's no need for anyone else to do that. I mean . . ." He broke off as Mr. Curry's face started to change color.

"I'll have you know, bear," he growled, "this is a very important event. There's a prize for the most original costume, so make sure you take good care of it. There are a lot of frills and I don't want any of them damaged. Otherwise it will be difficult to iron."

"Bears are good at frills, Mr. Curry," exclaimed Paddington, anxious to make amends. "If you like," he added recklessly, "I'll do a 'bob-a-job' for you and iron it when I do the rest of the laundry."

Mr. Curry stared at him. "Do you mean to say Mrs. Bird's allowing you to *iron* her laundry?" he exclaimed.

"Well," said Paddington truthfully, "it isn't so much that she's *letting* me, she says I *must* do it . . . *after* I've finished the mending."

Mr. Curry began to look more and more impressed, for Mrs. Bird's reputation as a housekeeper was second to none in the neighborhood. He gave another surreptitious glance in the direction of the Browns' house and then beckoned Paddington to come closer.

"If you like, bear," he said, lowering his voice so that no one else could overhear, "you can do it all in *my* house."

Mr. Curry licked his finger and then held it up in the air. "My shirt won't take long to dry in this breeze," he continued. "While you're finishing off some of your other jobs I'll set everything up for you so that it will be ready. There are one or two small holes which need darning. I was going to have them invisibly mended but if you use a mushroom you shouldn't find it too difficult."

"A *mushroom*, Mr. Curry?" repeated Paddington in surprise.

Mr. Curry looked at him suspiciously. "I trust you know what you're doing, bear?" he barked. "*Everyone* knows you need a mushroom when you're doing mending."

"Oh, yes, Mr. Curry," said Paddington hastily, as he caught sight of the gathering storm clouds on the face of the Browns' neighbor. "I'll get one from Mrs. Bird. I know where she keeps them."

"Hmm." Mr. Curry gave him another searching look and then carried on with his instructions about the various tasks he wanted done.

"I shall be out for the remainder of the afternoon," he said. "I have to see about the rest of my costume and I'm not sure how long it will take, but you can lay my shirt out ready for me to change into when I get back. In fact," he continued, "I have an even better idea. When you've finished you can take it straight to the Town Hall for me. I can change there and it'll save me coming back home again."

While Mr. Curry's voice droned on Paddington considered the matter. He was usually very wary about doing any odd jobs for the Browns' neighbor, especially ones which actually took place inside his house, but for once he couldn't see anything against the idea. In fact the more he thought about it the better it seemed, for his present run of luck at number thirty-two Windsor Gardens had been so bad it couldn't possibly get any worse.

Having reached the end of his instructions Mr. Curry paused in order to open up the gap in his fence. "If you make a good job of things," he said, "I *may* add a little something to your collection later."

"Thank you very much, Mr. Curry," said Paddington gratefully.

He cast a doubtful glance up the garden toward the Browns' kitchen as he clambered through the hole, but to his relief there was no one to be seen, and a moment later the board slipped back into place behind him.

Although he had almost convinced himself of the wisdom of his actions, Paddington had a nasty feeling that neither Mrs. Brown nor Mrs. Bird would entirely share his views.

Fortunately for their peace of mind, however, they were both much too busy with their cleaning to notice any of the comings and goings outside.

It wasn't until much later that same afternoon that Mrs. Bird suddenly paused in the middle of her household chores and looked out of the dining-room window with an air of surprise.

"That's funny," she said. "All the washing's gone. It was there a few minutes ago."

"Perhaps Paddington's taken it somewhere," said Mrs. Brown vaguely. "I saw him go past the window with a large pile just now." She frowned. "I wish he'd do one thing at a time. It was cooking just now—at least, I think it was. He was poking about in the vegetable basket looking for something."

A worried expression came over Mrs. Bird's face, for she was suddenly reminded of the fact that Paddington had also been searching for a needle and thread at one point. "I do hope he didn't take my lecture to heart this morning," she said. "I know I told him I expected to see the washing how I'd left it, but I didn't really mean for him to go to all that trouble. Where *can* he have gone with it?"

Despite her stern exterior, the Browns' housekeeper was a kindly soul at heart, and she began to look even more unhappy at the thought of Paddington taking her remarks amiss.

All the same, unhappy though Mrs. Bird looked, it was safe to say she would have looked even more disturbed had she been able to see the object of her thoughts at that particular moment.

For Paddington was in Mr. Curry's kitchen. Not only that, but he was in a mess. Far from things being better with a change of scene, they had become ten times worse than he could possibly have imagined in his wildest dreams.

He stared mournfully at Mr. Curry's ironing board. Or rather, to be strictly accurate, he directed his gaze toward a tightly compressed bundle of brown and white material which was lying in the middle, and from which rose a steady stream of dense, black smoke.

Picking up a wooden spoon which was lying nearby, he gingerly poked what was left of Mr. Curry's shirt and then stepped back hastily as another, even larger cloud rose from the smoldering embers.

Paddington sniffed the air unhappily. It was a strange smell; a mixture of steam, burnt cloth, and rotting vegetation. Worse still, it showed no signs of wanting to go away. Despite several goes with an air-freshener and opening the kitchen window to its widest extent, it continued to lie like some heavy jungle mist over the ironing board.

But it wasn't so much the smell that caused Paddington's woebegone look, it was the thought of how he was going to get out of his present difficulties.

Mr. Curry's shirt had started life as one of the collar-attached variety; now there was little if anything attached to it at all. The collar itself hung by a thread, rather as if it had been sewn on by an absent-minded tailor just before closing time.

Had he been asked to explain what had gone wrong, Paddington would have been hard put to sort matters

out in his own mind let alone put them into words.

The first big setback had been the iron. Although he'd often watched Mrs. Bird with her laundry he'd never actually done any ironing before, and it had all turned out much harder than he had expected. Mrs. Bird had an electric steam iron which positively glided over her laundry, hardly ever leaving the slightest trace of a singe, let alone any burn mark. Mr. Curry's iron, on the other hand, had to be heated first on the gas stove, and before he went out he demonstrated how to test it in order to make certain it was hot enough to use.

"The old-fashioned ways are the best, bear!" he

barked, and taking a mouthful of water he picked up the iron and blew spray all over the bottom, causing spluttering globules of water to bound off in all directions. "That's something my mother taught me."

Paddington had been so surprised at the thought of Mr. Curry having a mother he hadn't really concentrated on the rest of the lecture. As a result he missed what, if anything, the Browns' neighbor had to say on the subject of testing irons to make sure they weren't *too* hot.

In the event, either bears' spray was different from Mr. Curry's or he should have stuck to water instead of cocoa, for having made the iron extra specially hot in the hope of getting it right first time, Paddington found to his horror that it seemed intent on setting fire to anything and everything that happened to come within range.

Nothing was sacred; the cloth top on the ironing board; the plastic cover on the kitchen table; the linoleum; even the asbestos stand had gone a funny color.

In the end, with the safety of his whiskers very much in mind, he'd been forced to let go of the iron, as ill-luck would have it, right on top of Mr. Curry's shirt. It was then, as a strange sizzling noise filled the air, that he suddenly remembered he'd left a mushroom up one of the sleeves by mistake, and it was this that was giving off most of the smell.

He had been a bit doubtful about the mushroom right from the start, but Mr. Curry had been most insistent that it was the only proper way to mend things. Paddington found that having paws made sewing a bit difficult at the best of times, and either Mrs. Bird's mushrooms were extra soft or Mr. Curry was used to particularly hard ones, for he'd got through a whole pound in no time at all.

Paddington clambered on to Mr. Curry's kitchen stool and stared unhappily at the result of his labors.

Apart from the telltale mushroom stains, it would have taken a very short-sighted person indeed not to have spotted where the mending had taken place. Far from being invisible, it looked more like a relief map of the Himalayas.

The only good thing about it as far as he could see were the creases, which were certainly nice and sharp. Mr. Curry had mentioned his creases quite a few times, and he certainly wouldn't have had any cause to complain about the lack of them, for his shirt had the appearance of a squashed concertina. Unfortunately, though, that was where the resemblance ended, for when Paddington tried pulling it apart it made a most unmusical sound and several bits came away in his paw.

A hurried search through the kitchen drawers yielded a few well-worn dusters and a pile of old rags, but nothing remotely suitable for use as patches.

It was as he was gazing out of the window in search of inspiration that a faint gleam of hope suddenly appeared in Paddington's eyes. In the past he'd often found that some of his best ideas came at the very moment when things looked their blackest—almost as if they were intended, and although the present one was but a tiny flicker at the end of a very long tunnel, things were too desperate for it to be ignored.

A moment later there was a click from the back door as it shut behind him and for the second time that day the boards in Mr. Curry's fence parted and a familiar-looking hat followed by some equally familiar-looking whiskers appeared in the gap.

Paddington was about to put one of his plans into action and with the sun already sinking below the rooftops there was no time to be lost.

*

The Browns paused at the entrance to the Town Hall ballroom and braced themselves as they prepared to join the milling mass of people inside.

Mrs. Brown glanced anxiously over her shoulder. "Come along, Paddington," she called. "Keep with us, or you'll get lost."

"If he does we shall find him soon enough," said Mr. Brown gloomily. "Anyone can see who it is a mile away. I know it's a fancy-dress parade but does he *have* to wear dark glasses and a beard?"

"I don't think he's actually going in for anything, Henry," said Mrs. Brown vaguely. "He's just . . . well, he's just *wearing* them. I expect he's got his reasons."

"That," said Mr. Brown, "is what I'm afraid of."

Mrs. Brown lapsed into silence and exchanged anxious glances with the rest of the family. There was really no answer to Mr. Brown's question. At least, none that sprang readily to mind.

The fact of the matter was, Paddington had been behaving very strangely all the evening. On his return from wherever he'd been he had a quick bath without being asked, which was most unusual, and then he'd retired to his room armed with his disguise outfit. He'd stayed there with the curtains tightly drawn until it was time for supper, and when he'd finally emerged from his room wearing his beard and dark glasses, his hat had been pulled down very tightly over his face indeed.

"He hardly touched his Shepherd's Pie," remarked Mrs. Brown. "That's always a bad sign."

"He'll touch it soon enough when he's hungry," said Mrs. Bird darkly.

The Browns' housekeeper had her suspicions on the subject of Paddington's desire not to be recognized, but before she had a chance to say any more their attention was caught by a sudden commotion from the far side of the room.

"Mercy me!" cried Mrs. Bird, as a strange, white, billowing object clambered on to the stage. "Whatever is it?"

But like Mr. Brown before her, the Browns' housekeeper posed her question in vain, for the apparition was such a mixture of frills and bows and tapes and seemingly miles of cloth entangled with long pieces of cord, it beggared description.

It was so peculiar that even the Master of Ceremonies was momentarily at a loss for words, and it wasn't until he reached forward and poked his microphone through a flap in the front of the material that the awful truth suddenly dawned on the Browns.

"What a good idea coming as a tent," said the Master of Ceremonies, silencing the applause with a wave of his other hand. "What gave you the idea?"

"Tent?" came a muffled, but all-too-familiar voice. *"Tent?* How dare you! I'll give you tent!"

The red face of Mr. Curry emerged from the folds and glared toward the audience. "Bear!" he bellowed. "Are you in the hall, bear? If you are, come up here at once. I'll teach you to mend my best shirt with a tent! I'll . . . I'll . . ."

The Master of Ceremonies looked slightly put out as he jumped back in alarm and found he'd entangled his microphone lead with what seemed to be a lot of guy ropes. "I only wanted to congratulate you on winning first prize," he said. "There's no need to be like that."

"What's that?" It was Mr. Curry's turn to be taken aback. "Did you say *first* prize?"

"That's right." The Master of Ceremonies recovered his composure. "Yours is one of the most original entries I've seen for a long time. But as it now appears to have been a joint effort I think we shall have to split the prize down the middle."

"I'm having my joint split down the middle!" exclaimed a voice behind the Browns. They turned just in time to see Paddington coming out from beneath a table where he had been hiding. He was looking most upset.

"No, dear," said Mrs. Brown hastily. "You haven't actually won a joint. Mr. Curry's won some money and the man in charge has very kindly suggested he shares it with you."

"If I were you I'd go up and get your half while you've got the chance," broke in Jonathan. "You may never see it otherwise."

Paddington needed no second bidding, and he hurried up to the platform as fast as his legs would carry him.

"I'm sorry about the guy ropes, Mr. Curry," he called, as he positioned himself as far away from the Browns' neighbor as possible. "I'm afraid I left them on by mistake."

"Er, yes," said the Master of Ceremonies. "Quite. Now"— he pointed the microphone toward Paddington—"tell me, what do you plan to do with your half of the money?"

Paddington raised his hat politely. "I'm giving it to the Home for Retired Bears in Lima," he announced. "That's what I was collecting it for in the first place."

"What a nice idea," said the M.C. over the applause. "But won't you be keeping *any* for yourself?"

Paddington removed his beard while he considered the matter. What with one thing and another he'd had a very hard week doing his jobs and until now there had been absolutely nothing to show for it.

"I think," he announced at last, "I may keep Mr. Curry's bob."

The Browns' neighbor stared at him in astonishment. "My *what*?" he gasped.

Paddington hastily put his beard back on and took a deep breath before replying. "Your bob, Mr. Curry," he said. "The one you promised me for doing your ironing."

If Mr. Curry's face had been like thunder before, it grew positively purple with rage as Paddington's words sank in. For a second or two he looked as if he was about to stomp off the stage. Then he hesitated as a loud shout of "Give him the money" rang out. Paddington was a well-known figure in the Portobello Market and over the years he'd gained a good many friends among the street traders, quite a few of whom were present and only too happy to take up the cry.

"Quite right, too," said Mrs. Bird, trying to keep the note of pleasure from her voice as with a great deal of ill grace Mr. Curry began feeling inside his shirt. "I'm not given to betting, but if I had to put a shirt on anyone's back it would be Paddington's rather than Mr. Curry's. One way and another bears do have a habit of coming out on top in the end—I'm *very* pleased to say."

CHAPTER FIVE

Paddington Gets a Rise

"ONE POUND EIGHTY-NINE PENCE!" exclaimed Paddington. "Just to say 'Congratulations'!" He grabbed the edge of the Post Office counter as he nearly fell backwards off his suitcase with surprise. "But it's only one word!"

The lady behind the window gave a superior sniff. "You don't get something for nothing in this world," she said severely. "Especially when it comes to sending telegrams."

Paddington gazed up at her, adding one of his special

hard stares for good measure. As far as he was concerned he felt so aggrieved he would have liked nothing
better than to send the Post Office a telegram congratu-
lating them on being able to charge so much, but he
thought better of it, for it sounded a very expensive
way of complaining.

"Anyway," said the lady, wilting slightly under his
unblinking gaze, "it isn't only *one* word—it's seventeen.
We charge extra for the address, you know."

She put on her superior face again as she pushed
Paddington's piece of paper across the counter and
jabbed at it with a pencil. "Talking of which, I rather
feel we have a few unnecessary words here, don't you?
'MR. HENRY BROWN,'" she read, "'NUMBER THIRTY-
TWO WINDSOR GARDENS, LONDON, ENGLAND,
EUROPE, THE WORLD, THE UNIVERSE. CONGRATULA-
TIONS. PADDINGTON.'"

Paddington gave the lady an even harder stare. "*We*
wanted to make sure it got there," he said firmly, and
taking the piece of paper from under the grille he
opened his suitcase, placed it in the secret compartment, and after raising his hat politely, left the building.

Paddington had never sent a telegram before and as
far as he was concerned he wasn't likely to in the future
either—not even if the Post Office paid him to do so.

All of which, however, didn't go very far toward

solving his immediate problem; in fact it only made it worse.

It had to do with the fact that Mr. Brown's birthday was looming up, and for one reason and another he hadn't done a thing about it. Apart from anything else, Mr. Brown wasn't very easy to buy presents for—especially if you didn't have much pocket money.

Although he was much too polite to mention the matter, Paddington hadn't had a rise in his pocket money ever since he'd first gone to live with the Browns. Luckily, extras in the way of Christmas and birthday presents helped matters along, not to mention the odd sums he earned from time to time. But the years had seen a steady increase in the price of buns, and although he never really wanted for anything, it wasn't always easy to make both ends meet.

However, in the circumstances, it hardly seemed the right moment to bring the matter up, so he'd been driven to trying to think up unusual but cheap ways of wishing Mr. Brown a Happy Birthday.

He'd already made a special card, and the idea of sending a Greetings telegram as well had come to him one morning when he'd seen an advertisement on a hoarding in the market. According to the advertisement it was a very inexpensive way of making people feel happy, and at the time it had seemed like a very good idea indeed; now, his hopes had received a severe setback.

Paddington decided to consult his friend Mr. Gruber on the subject. Mr. Gruber was good at solving life's problems, and even if he didn't come up with an answer straight away he had a happy knack of making things seem better than they were at first sight.

Having directed another hard stare at the outside of the Post Office, he set off in the direction of the market, his duffle-coat hood pulled well up over the top of his hat in order to keep out the chill morning air.

In the space of a few days a change had come over the weather and autumn had given way to winter with a vengeance; so much so that Paddington rather wished he'd plucked up courage to tell Mrs. Bird that he'd used his best Wellingtons during his cooking exploits at Luckham House.

His old ones had long since seen better days, and the first flakes of the winter snow were already seeping through some gaps in the bottom, making the fur round his toes quite soggy.

It was while he was sheltering in a doorway not far from the Portobello Road, nibbling a much-needed sandwich before completing the remainder of his journey, that Paddington's eye suddenly alighted on a notice pinned to the door itself.

It said, quite simply: MR. ROMNEY MARSH, R.A. LIFE CLASSES. PORTRAIT PAINTING A SPECIALITY. MODEL WANTED—URGENTLY. TOP RATES PAID.

It didn't take Paddington long to make up his mind. It seemed too good an opportunity to miss, and a moment later found him hurrying up the stairs as fast as his legs would carry him.

Mr. Marsh's studio was at the top of the building,

and as Paddington knocked on the door and entered he gazed around with interest. Apart from the walls it was not unlike being inside an enormous greenhouse, for almost the entire roof area was glassed in. In the center of the room there was a platform with a small table on which stood a bowl of fruit, while to one side there was an unlit coke stove around which sat a small group of people with easels.

It was yet another reminder to Paddington of his visit to Luckham House, for it wasn't unlike the scene from the opera he'd listened to, although from the way some of the students were holding their brushes their hands weren't simply frozen with the cold, they were totally without feeling.

Mr. Marsh himself was obviously made of sterner stuff, for unlike his students who were all wearing overcoats, he was clad quite simply in a large flowing smock which billowed out behind him as he caught sight of Paddington and crossed the room to bid him welcome.

"My dear sir," he announced. "Welcome to our little gathering. Have you come to enroll?"

Paddington raised his hat politely as he shook Mr. Marsh's outstretched hand with his other paw. "No, thank you," he announced. "I've just had a marmalade sandwich."

"Oh! Oh, dear me!" Mr. Marsh gave a nervous giggle.

"In that case . . . er . . . what can we do for you?"

"I'd like to be a model if I may," said Paddington.

"A model what?" said a gloomy voice from somewhere among the students.

"Silence!" Mr. Marsh raised his hand imperiously as he joined Paddington in giving the group a hard stare. "This is not a laughing matter. Stop that tittering at once."

He whirled back to address Paddington. "You couldn't have come at a more opportune moment," he exclaimed, as he led Paddington toward the platform. "Between you and me," he whispered, "we're getting a little tired of painting fruit. Besides, it's so expensive at this time of the year and you only have to turn your back for a moment and you find someone's eaten it."

He placed Paddington in the center of the platform alongside the table and then stood back, holding his brush at arm's length and eyeing it through half-closed eyes in order to size up the situation.

"Let me tell you," he said, turning to his class, "that anyone who captures those whiskers in oils will have their work cut out."

"Capture my whiskers in oils!" exclaimed Paddington. "But they're not even loose."

"We shall need our burnt umber," continued Romney Marsh, ignoring the interruption, "with perhaps a touch of orange madder here and there. Some of the stains are really quite remarkable in their depth of color." He stroked his beard thoughtfully. "Black for the nose, obviously . . . and the mouth. I would suggest forest green for the tongue . . ."

"Forest green!" cried Paddington in alarm. He peered at his reflection in a nearby full-length mirror and then his face cleared. "That's not my *real* tongue," he said thankfully. "I expect it's where I licked the end of my pen when I tried to send a telegram this morning."

"Er . . . yes . . . quite!" Mr. Marsh came back down to earth with a bump as he realized Paddington was talking to him. "Now, would you mind removing your duffle coat, please? After all, this *is* supposed to be a life class. Perhaps you could pretend you're sunbathing on the beach or something?" he added brightly.

Paddington considered the matter for a moment. All in all, he had quite a good imagination when he put his mind to it, but as he gazed round the unheated studio try as he might he couldn't even begin to picture the kind of scene Mr. Marsh obviously had in mind; and he certainly had no intention of taking off his duffle coat.

"Bears don't do sunbathing," he said firmly. "They do *shade* bathing instead. I think I'll keep it on if you don't mind."

Romney Marsh clucked impatiently. "I suppose we mustn't look a gift horse in the mouth," he said. "One has to take what one can get these days, but *really*!

"We'll just have to pretend you're some kind of statue." He eyed Paddington's old Wellingtons doubtfully as he began arranging him in a suitable pose. "Some of you may have trouble with the legs. It's hard to tell where they begin let alone where they end up. Still," he gave a sigh, "life is nothing without a challenge.

"Now," he continued, addressing Paddington as he stood back in order to view his handiwork, "whatever you do—don't move. I want you to keep absolutely still."

Paddington did as he was bidden and for the next few minutes, apart from some movement in the class itself as the members took up new positions in order to get the best view of their latest subject, all was quiet.

To start with Paddington felt quite pleased with his new occupation. Although he had often heard Mrs. Bird grumble about the way some people seemed to get paid for nothing, he'd never heard of anyone being paid to stand absolutely still while they did it, and it seemed very good value indeed.

But gradually, as time went by, he began to wish more and more that he'd taken up Mr. Marsh's first suggestion and pretended he was sunbathing. Practically any kind of pose would have been better than the one he'd finally ended up with, but making believe he was lying on a beach enjoying the sunshine sounded nicest of all in the circumstances. As it was he felt more like a ballet dancer who'd got a bad attack of cramp while trying to execute a particularly difficult movement. The only time he could remember feeling quite so uncomfortable was when he'd been caught unawares in a waxworks museum, and that had only lasted a matter of minutes, whereas Mr. Marsh's class showed every sign of going on forever. From the little he could see out of the corner of his eye most of them were still busy with their charcoals making preliminary sketches, and even Romney Marsh himself had only just started on his burnt umber.

To make matters worse, a fly was beginning to take more than a passing interest in him. Paddington had often wondered where flies went in the winter time, now he knew. It circled round him several times trying to make up its mind, and then, unable to resist the attraction of some marmalade which had accidentally got left on his whiskers, it landed on the end of his nose.

Paddington could stand it no longer. Taking advantage of a moment when everyone seemed to have their

heads bent over their easels, he lowered one paw, brushed his whiskers clean and gave a swipe at the offending fly at the same time. Then he tried to resume his former position.

But if Paddington thought his movement would go unnoticed he was doomed to disappointment. The howl of protest which went up from the class couldn't have been any louder if he'd gone out for a walk, done his shopping in the market, and then returned after a hearty lunch.

"That takes the biscuit!" exclaimed a student bitterly, pointing to his canvas. "I'd just got the folds in his duffle coat right—now look at it!"

"His whiskers are pointing a different way too," said another voice. "*And* some of them have changed color. They were all orange to begin with."

Romney Marsh's beard quivered with indignation. "It's too bad," he said. "Twenty pence an hour I'm paying, and look what happens . . ."

"Twenty pence an *hour*!" exclaimed Paddington hotly. "But your card said you pay top rates."

"That," said Mr. Marsh, drawing himself up to his full height, "is for professional models. We don't give it to every Tom, Dick, or bear who happens to drop in on the off-chance. Anyway," he added, "if you come every day for a week until the pictures are finished it'll soon add up."

"Every day for a *week*!" Paddington stared at Romney Marsh as if he could hardly believe his eyes let alone his ears. It had been a bad enough experience until then, but the thought of it carrying on for another four days was hard to contemplate, and he decided to take matters into his own paws without further ado.

But as he tried to bend down to pick up his bag Paddington made yet another discovery. Standing for a long time was one thing; trying to move off again afterward was another matter again. What with the cold of the studio and the lack of circulation, his legs positively refused to cooperate. As he began to topple he clutched wildly at the nearest available object, and for a second or two it held him. Then it began to slide and a moment later everything in the room seemed to turn upside down and round about as he fell to the floor, with first the bowl of fruit, then the table on top of him.

For a while Paddington lay where he was with his eyes tightly shut, hardly daring to breathe, and then gradually he became aware of voices as everybody crowded round to give assistance.

"Perhaps you'd better give him the kiss of life?" suggested one of the students.

Mr. Marsh eyed the recumbent form distastefully as he removed the table. Although Paddington had managed to wipe most of the marmalade from his whiskers, there were still a few traces, and these had now been added to by a number of squashed grapes and the remains of a pear.

"I'm afraid I'm not very good at first aid," he said hastily. "I think perhaps I'd better have some volunteers.

"All right," he said crossly, when no one moved. "*One* volunteer. Surely there's *someone* who knows about these things."

But Romney Marsh needn't have bothered. Paddington wiggled himself several times to make sure he was still working, and having decided he was in one piece after all, he jumped to his feet and made off down the stairs as fast as he could go.

His legs might not have been in peak condition, but they were still capable of a good turn of speed, and they didn't stop until he arrived outside Mr. Gruber's and there they propelled him, still panting, on to the horsehair sofa inside the shop.

If Mr. Gruber was surprised by the sudden arrival of his friend he showed no sign, and while Paddington got his breath back and began relating the story of the morning's events, he busied himself on the small stove he kept at the back of the shop, making the cocoa for their elevenses.

"I daresay you could do with this, Mr. Brown," he said a bit later, when he arrived carrying two steaming mugs and set them down on the table in front of the sofa. "I know Mr. Marsh's studio of old and it's one of the coldest spots in the Portobello Road.

"I must say," he continued, as he sat down alongside his friend, "making both ends meet can be a bit of a problem at times—especially if you don't get your sums right."

"Oh, I'm always very careful with my accounts, Mr. Gruber," said Paddington. "I do them every night before I go to bed."

"I daresay," said Mr. Gruber, "and I'm sure you're very good at it, Mr. Brown. But then, it's like saying 'how long is a piece of string?' or 'what does two and two make?' The answer is 'it all depends.' You can prove almost anything by mathematics."

Mr. Gruber stirred his cocoa thoughtfully. "Your story reminds me of an old music hall joke in which it's proved that a man can work for three hundred and sixty-five days in a year and yet, with holidays and weekends, work no time at all. It's so long ago since I saw it I've forgotten the details, but in much the same way I could prove to you that you are actually better off now by eighty-nine pence than when you set out this morning.

"The fact is, Mr. Brown," he continued, "if you had worked as a model at Mr. Marsh's studio for an hour a day at twenty pence an hour, in one week you would have earned one pound, but you didn't, so you are one pound worse off, right?"

Paddington nodded his agreement from behind a cloud of cocoa steam.

"On the other hand, if you had sent Mr. Brown his

telegram it would have cost you one pound eighty-nine pence, but you didn't, so you are one pound eighty-nine pence better off, right?"

Paddington thought the matter over and then nodded his agreement yet again.

"In that case," said Mr. Gruber, "even if you take away the first pound you are still eighty-nine pence better off." He reached over and held up a bun to Paddington with one hand while tapping his open duffle coat pocket with the other. "To prove I'm right, Mr. Brown," he said with a twinkle in his eye, "try feeling in there."

Paddington did as his friend suggested and then nearly dropped his cocoa with astonishment as his paw touched some coins. They certainly hadn't been there that morning, and yet when he took them out and counted them they came to exactly eighty-nine pence. It was all most mysterious.

Mr. Gruber chuckled when he saw the look on Paddington's face. "Sometimes mathematics has to do with conjuring as well," he said.

"Perhaps I could send Mr. Brown a very *short* telegram?" exclaimed Paddington excitedly.

Mr. Gruber shook his head. "If I were you I would keep it, Mr. Brown," he said. "Besides, I have a much better idea. One which I'm sure will be appreciated even more. It has to do with something I came across years ago when I was in America, and if you like I will tell you all about it . . ."

*

"Cats!" exclaimed Mr. Brown bitterly. "Why is it they always wait until you're fast asleep before they make a din?" He switched on the bedside light and focused his eyes on the alarm clock. "One minute past twelve! Anyone would think they've been waiting for midnight. Right outside our front door, too!"

Mrs. Brown sat up rubbing her eyes. "Where are you going, Henry?" she called.

Mr. Brown paused at the bedroom door. "To fetch a jug of cold water," he said grimly. "It happens to be my birthday today and I want to make the most of it."

"Just listen!" he exclaimed, as he came back into the room. "Have you ever heard anything like it?"

Mrs. Brown hesitated. Now that it had been mentioned there *was* something vaguely familiar about the noise outside. It had a kind of rhythm to it, a beginning and an end, which reminded her of something.

"Careful, Henry," she called, as Mr. Brown started to open the window. "I don't think that's a cat. I think it's someone singing."

"Singing?" echoed Mr. Brown. "*Singing*? I'll give them singing if I catch them. Don't tell me it's carol singers already. I know they get earlier and earlier each year, but this is ridiculous."

Mrs. Brown gave a sigh as her husband's voice disappeared down the stairs. Then she got out of bed, put on her dressing-gown, and joined the rest of the family on the landing as they too appeared, wakened by all the noise.

Paddington looked most upset when Mr. Brown flung open the front door and he heard what he'd been mistaken for.

"I'm not a *cat*, Mr. Brown," he exclaimed. "I'm a singing telegram boy. They used to have them in America and they kept them for very special occasions."

And to show what he meant he launched into yet another verse of "Happy Birthday."

Mr. Brown went quite pink about the ears. "Er . . . yes, well . . . thank you very much, Paddington," he said. "It's very kind of you, I'm sure. Most unusual."

"Oh, it wasn't really my idea," admitted Paddington. "It was Mr. Gruber's. He told me all about it."

"Mr. Gruber's idea it may have been," said Mrs. Bird briskly, as she took charge of the situation. "But I doubt very much if he intended you delivering your telegram tonight, so upstairs with you. It's time certain bears were tucked up in bed. And that goes for the rest of us too."

"Er . . . before you go," Mr. Brown called after the retreating figure of Paddington. "You might like to know I've decided to put you on my birthday honors list."

Paddington peered down at the others over the top of the banisters. "Your birthday honors list, Mr. Brown?" he exclaimed in surprise. "I thought only the Queen had those."

"Well, *I'm* having one this year," said Mr. Brown grandly. "I've decided to give you a rise in your pocket money. I'm told you haven't had one since you came, so there's a lot to be made up. We'll talk about it in the morning."

"Henry!" said Mrs. Brown some while later, as a very excited Paddington at last made his way up to bed. "How awful! Fancy us forgetting a thing like that. What ever made you think of it?"

"A little bird told me," said Mr. Brown vaguely.

"A *little* bird?" chorused Jonathan and Judy.

"Well, maybe it's not so little," admitted Mr. Brown. "It's called the Gruber bird. Wise as an owl, knowledgeable as a Secretary bird, and very good on the telephone.

"He rang me earlier this evening and mentioned it to me. Very politely, of course, and full of apologies. But he's absolutely right."

He glanced up the stairs, but Paddington had already disappeared from view in the direction of his room. He had a lot on his mind and he wanted to write it all down in his scrap book before it disappeared. As for his rise; that demanded a very special postcard indeed to his Aunt Lucy in Peru—one of the giant ones from the stationers in the market.

"I still can't think how it ever came about," said Mrs. Brown.

"Perhaps," said Mrs. Bird, as she joined the others at the foot of the stairs, "it's because we often take for granted the things that mean the most to us.

"Something we should never, *ever* do," she added, amid general agreement, "especially when it comes to bears."

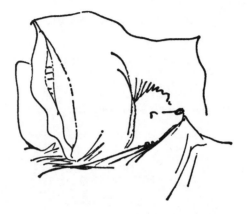

CHAPTER SIX

Mr. Curry Lets Off Steam

ON THE MORNING OF Mr. Brown's birthday Paddington overslept, which was most unusual. When he did finally emerge from his slumbers it was to the sound of a strange knocking noise. At first he thought it was to do with a dream he'd been having; all about a woodpecker which had accidentally got trapped inside his hat. But his hat was still lying on the dressing table where he'd left it the night before, and when he felt his head it didn't show any signs of having been pecked.

In any case, having rubbed his eyes several times to

make doubly sure he was properly awake, he discovered the noise hadn't stopped. If anything it seemed to be getting worse, and it appeared to be coming from somewhere outside.

Paddington hurried to his bedroom window and peered out. As he did so he nearly fell over backwards with surprise, for while he'd been asleep a strange-looking wooden hut had appeared in the garden. It was standing in the middle of the snow-covered cabbage patch, and as far as he could make out it had no windows at all, although it made up for this by having a short chimney, out of which rose a thin column of steam.

The noise was being caused by two workmen who were busy putting some finishing touches to the flat roof, and as one of them paused in order to rest from his hammering he looked up and caught sight of Paddington.

"You wait till this 'eats up properly, mate," he called. "It'll take the cobwebs out of your whiskers and no mistake."

Paddington had never heard of a hut for removing cobwebs before, so he put on his duffle coat and after a quick look at his own whiskers in the bathroom mirror, hurried downstairs in order to tell the others.

Mrs. Brown and Mrs. Bird exchanged uneasy glances

as he burst into the dining-room. Knowing how keen Paddington was on trying things out, they had been hoping to keep the whole matter a secret until the last possible moment.

"It's Daddy's birthday present," explained Judy. "It's what's known as a Sauna bath."

"It's meant to be a surprise," added Jonathan. "That's why the workmen are in such a hurry. We want to get it ready and working by the time he gets home."

Paddington listened carefully while the others explained all about Sauna baths and how they worked.

"You see," said Judy, "you have lots of large stones which you stand on a special place inside the hut. You heat them up and then pour cold water over them and it turns into steam. It's supposed to be very good for you. It opens up all the pores."

"In some parts of the world they even beat you with birch twigs afterward," added Jonathan. "It gives you a nice glow. Dad keeps on about wanting to lose weight—that's why we've bought it for him."

Paddington considered the matter for a moment. He'd never heard of anyone having a bath as a birthday present before, and although he was quite sure Mr. Brown would be surprised by it all, being soaked in steam and then beaten by birch twigs didn't seem a very good way of celebrating the occasion.

All the same, it definitely sounded worth investigating, even if he didn't actually test it out.

"Perhaps," he announced, "I'll just have a look through the keyhole, otherwise my whiskers might go soggy."

"Very wise," said Mrs. Bird. "Not that a Sauna bath mightn't do certain of those amongst us some good," she added meaningly, as Paddington donned his Wellington boots. "Mr. Brown isn't the only one who could do with losing a few pounds."

Paddington looked most offended at this last remark,

but as he hurried out into the garden he quickly forgot about it in his excitement.

By the time he reached the hut the workmen had already left, but they had obviously got the stones in a state of readiness for Mr. Brown's homecoming. Steam was billowing out through the chimney and from odd cracks in the woodwork. In fact, the whole thing looked rather like some primitive space machine a few moments before launching.

Paddington approached it gingerly and was about to apply his eye to a knothole which was low down in the door and looked slightly less steamy than the rest, when he heard a familiar voice bark out his name.

He jumped to his feet and as he turned round he saw to his dismay that Mr. Curry was gazing at him over the top of the fence.

"What's going on, bear?" demanded Mr. Curry. "Was that you making all that noise just now?"

"Oh, no, Mr. Curry," said Paddington hastily. "It woke *me* up. I was asleep too."

"Asleep!" exclaimed Mr. Curry. "I wasn't *asleep*. I never sleep." He gazed suspiciously across the fence. "What's that monstrosity? And what's all that smoke doing? It ought not to be allowed. I've a good mind to report it."

"Oh, that isn't *smoke*, Mr. Curry," said Paddington

knowledgeably. "That's steam. It's a special birthday surprise for Mr. Brown. It's what's known as a Sauna bath."

"A Sauna bath, eh?" Mr. Curry took a closer look at the hut.

"It's supposed to be very good for you," said Paddington, warming to his subject as he went on to repeat all that he'd been told about the matter.

"Very interesting, bear," said Mr. Curry when he'd finished. "Very interesting indeed. You say it's all ready to use?"

Paddington nodded. "They've heated the stones specially," he explained. "*And* they've put some cold water on to make the steam. Look . . ." He opened the door slightly to show the Browns' neighbor what he meant.

"Thank you very much, bear," said Mr. Curry unexpectedly. "That's very kind of you. I've always wanted to try one. I'll go in and change now."

Paddington's jaw dropped as the Browns' neighbor disappeared from view. He was used to Mr. Curry's habit of twisting other people's words to suit his own ends, but never in his wildest dreams had he meant to invite him over.

"The cheek of it!" exclaimed Mrs. Bird when she heard the news. "That's typical of Mr. Curry—always poking his nose in and wanting to get something for nothing."

"He'll get steam up his nose if he pokes it in there," said Jonathan, glancing out of the window.

"I hope he doesn't let it all out," said Judy. "Daddy *must* be the first one to try it. After all, it's *his* present."

A feeling of indignation ran round the Browns' dining-room. They had gone to great lengths to keep Mr. Brown's present from him until it was ready, even to the extent of persuading him to go into work that morning instead of taking the whole day off as he usually did, and they had no wish to spoil his homecoming by indulging in an argument with Mr. Curry.

"We should have put a padlock on the door," said Mrs. Brown. "I don't know why I didn't think of it at the time."

While the others were talking a thoughtful expression gradually crept over Paddington's face. Opening up his suitcase he felt inside the secret compartment and withdrew a small parcel done up in brightly colored wrapping paper.

"Perhaps," he announced, "you could use *my* present to Mr. Brown?" And to everyone's astonishment he unwrapped the paper and held up a small silvery object.

"I *was* going to send a telegram as a surprise," he said, "but I had a bit of trouble, so I bought this instead. It was really meant for his tool shed, but I expect it will look much better on a Sauna bath—especially a new one."

"Gosh!" said Jonathan enviously, as he examined Paddington's present. "It's a special combination lock. I bet Dad'll be pleased."

"Just so long as he doesn't forget the number," said Mrs. Brown nervously. "You know what he's like when it comes to things like that. It would be awful if he couldn't get the door open on the first day."

"It's all right, Mrs. Brown," said Paddington. He looked round carefully to make sure no one else could overhear. "The man in the shop adjusted it specially so that it used my birthday date. He said that way we would never forget."

"A good idea," said Mrs. Bird approvingly. "And if you want my advice you'll put it on the door straight away. It'll stop Mr. Curry taking advantage."

Paddington needed no second bidding and a few seconds later he hurried back down the garden path again as fast as his legs would carry him. There was already a hasp on the door and it was a moment's work to push the flap home and slip the padlock into place. As he squeezed the two halves together they met with a satisfying click. He twiddled the various sets of numbers several times with his paws, just as the man in the shop had shown him, and then stood back breathing heavily, before testing it once more to make sure all was well.

It had been a race against time, but in the circumstances Paddington felt sure Mr. Brown would be more than pleased with his extra present. He could still hardly believe his good fortune at having chosen something which worked in so well with the Browns' gift, for no matter how hard he pulled the padlock it showed no sign of coming apart again.

The heat from the Sauna was slightly overpowering, and it was as he moved away in order to mop his brow that a puzzled expression came over Paddington's face. It was very strange, but it was almost as if he could hear a repetition of the knocking which had woken him earlier in the day.

Admittedly it was rather more muffled than it had been before, but it was getting louder with every passing moment, and it seemed to be coming from *inside* the hut. In fact, even as he watched, the door began to shake, just as if someone was rattling it from the other side.

He gave the door a couple of taps with his paw. "Excuse me," he called. "Is anyone there?"

Paddington wasn't quite sure what, if anything, he expected by way of a reply, but in the event he nearly jumped out of his skin with surprise.

"Yes, there is!" bellowed an all-too-familiar voice. "Is that you, bear? Let me out at once!"

Paddington gazed at the door in alarm. It hadn't occurred to him for one moment that Mr. Curry might have beaten him to it.

Recovering in double quick time he took hold of the padlock. "Coming, Mr. Curry," he called. "Don't worry. I've only got to set up my birthday date."

"Your *what*?" shouted Mr. Curry.

"My birthday date," called Paddington. "It's the twenty-fifth of June."

Paddington's words were the signal for a renewed burst of banging on the door. "But it's not the twenty-fifth of June," roared Mr. Curry. "That was months ago. And it's not *your* birthday. It's Mr. Brown's!"

But Paddington wasn't listening. Instead he gazed unhappily at the door. He couldn't remember ever having seen one quite so tightly shut before. Even allowing for the fact that Mr. Curry wasn't exactly helping matters by banging it, something seemed to have gone very wrong with the lock. No matter how hard he pulled, the two halves showed no sign whatsoever of coming apart.

"I shan't be long, Mr. Curry," he gasped, giving the lock one more tug. "It's a bit difficult with paws and the steam keeps going in my eyes . . ."

"The steam keeps going in *your* eyes!" bellowed Mr. Curry. "What do you think's happening to mine? I'm being boiled alive in here!"

Bending down, Paddington peered through the knothole he'd used earlier that morning. At first it was difficult to make out anything through the steam, but as his eyes grew accustomed to the gloom he gradually made out the shape of the Browns' neighbor. Even through the haze he could see what Mr. Curry meant. During the short space of time he'd been locked inside the hut, he'd taken on the appearance of an over-boiled lobster. A lobster, moreover, which was jumping up and down and showing every sign of wanting to get its pincers on the person responsible for its present condition.

Paddington looked round for help, but there wasn't a soul in sight. In desperation he opened his suitcase to see if there were any instructions which went with the lock, but apart from several testimonials on the outside of the box—all saying how impossible it was to open once it had been set—there was nothing at all.

As he gazed mournfully at his own lock Paddington felt he could have written a very good testimonial himself at that moment, and given a tape recorder he could have provided some appropriate sound effects to go with it into the bargain as well.

He rummaged through the suitcase again. "Would you like an old marmalade sandwich to be going on with, Mr. Curry?" he called. "I expect I could push some bits through one of the holes."

Paddington was a hopeful bear at heart, but even he had to admit that if Mr. Curry's reply was anything to go by, the market for sandwiches was at a particularly low ebb at that moment.

It was as he was about to close the lid of his suitcase that his gaze alighted on an object lying in the bottom. Over the years Paddington had collected quite a number of souvenirs, and he usually carried a selection of the more important ones around with him. By a strange coincidence the particular one which had just caught his eye had been given to him some years before when he'd visited Mr. Curry in hospital.

It was a stethoscope, and seeing it reminded him of a film he'd recently seen on television, all about a famous safe-breaker called "Lobes" Lavone. In the film no lock had been too complicated for Mr. Lavone. A few moments on his own with a stethoscope and even the toughest of strongroom doors would swing open to reveal its secrets. It had been a most exciting program and before he'd gone to bed that night Paddington had spent some time testing his own stethoscope on the Browns' front door. However, he'd never actually tried it out on a real combination lock before and it seemed a very good opportunity.

Paddington donned the ear-pieces as fast as he could, and then began twiddling the numbers while he applied the business end of the stethoscope to the lock. As he did so his face fell. Apart from the background music which always accompanied his escapades, Mr. Lavone insisted on working in complete silence. In fact, he got very cross if anyone so much as dared to breathe within earshot, whereas, heard through the ear-pieces, Mr. Curry's wheezing sounded not unlike a herd of elephants trying to get over a heavy cold. Far from being able to detect any telltale clicks, all Paddington could hear was the sound of banging and crashing as the Browns' neighbor stomped about inside the hut.

Taking advantage of a sudden lull, he was about to have one final go when his eardrums were nearly punctured by an unusually loud bellow from what seemed like two inches away.

"I can see you, bear!" roared Mr. Curry. "What are you doing now? Listening to the radio? How dare you at a time like this?"

Paddington dropped his stethoscope like a hot potato. "I wasn't listening to the radio, Mr. Curry," he called. "I was having trouble with my combinations."

"Your *combinations*?" The Browns' neighbor sounded as if he could hardly believe his ears. "I'll give you combinations!"

Paddington looked round hopefully for inspiration. "Stay where you are, Mr. Curry," he called. "I'll think of something."

"Stay where I am!" spluttered Mr. Curry. "*Stay where I am!* I can't do anything else, thanks to you. It's disgraceful. I'm being boiled alive. Call the Fire Brigade. Oooh! Help!"

But Mr. Curry's cries fell on deaf ears, for Paddington was already halfway up the garden. Desperate situations demanded desperate measures, and something Mr. Curry said had triggered off an idea in his mind.

Mrs. Brown glanced out into the garden and as she did so a puzzled look came over her face. "What on earth is that bear up to now?" she exclaimed.

As the others joined her at the dining-room window she pointed toward a small figure clad in a duffle coat and hat struggling to prop a ladder against the side of the Sauna hut.

"And what's he doing with my best plastic bucket?" demanded Mrs. Bird.

If the Browns' housekeeper was expecting an answer from the others to her question, she was disappointed, for they were as mystified as she was. In any case they were saved the trouble, for almost before she had finished speaking Paddington had climbed up the ladder and was crawling across the roof of the hut as if his very life depended on it. Before their astonished gaze, he filled the bucket with snow and then removed the cowl from the top of the chimney and began pouring the contents down the open end.

As he did so the column of steam which rose from the hole surpassed anything that had gone before. For a moment or two Paddington completely disappeared from view. Then, as the mist gradually cleared, he once again came into view looking, if anything, even more worried than he had before.

As a distant roar of rage followed by the sound of

renewed banging came from somewhere inside the hut
Jonathan and Judy looked at each other. The same
thought was in both their minds.

"Come on," said Jonathan. "If you ask me,
Paddington's in trouble!"

"And what," called Mrs. Bird, as she hurried down
the garden path after the others, "do you think you're
doing up there? You'll catch your death of cold in all
that steam."

Paddington peered down unhappily from the roof of the Sauna hut. "I think I've shut Mr. Curry inside by mistake, Mrs. Bird," he announced. "I think something's gone wrong with my padlock."

"Crumbs! Let me have a go." Jonathan took hold of the lock and began twiddling the dials as a sudden thought struck him. Almost at once there was a satisfying click and to everyone's surprise the two halves parted. "Stand by for blasting!" he called, as he removed the lock from the hasp and the door swung open.

The others waited with bated breath to hear what Mr. Curry would have to say as he emerged from the hut. Far from losing weight he seemed to have gained several pounds as he swelled up in anger at the sight of the Browns. Then, just as he opened his mouth in order to let forth, he gave a shiver and pulled his towel tightly round himself as a sudden draught of cold air caught him unawares. In the end all he could manage was a loud "Brrrrrrr!"

"Perhaps I could beat you with birch twigs, Mr. Curry?" called Paddington hopefully. "I expect bears are good at that and it'll warm you up."

As he peered over the edge of the roof a lump of snow detached itself from his hat and landed fairly and squarely on top of Mr. Curry's head.

"Bah!" The Browns' neighbor found his voice at last. "Come down here at once, bear. Wait until I get dressed. I'll . . . I'll . . ."

Mrs. Bird took a firm grip of her broom handle. "You'll *what*?" she asked.

Mr. Curry swelled up again and opened his mouth as if he was about to say something. Then he thought better of it and a moment later he stalked off and disappeared through the hole in the fence.

"Thank goodness for that!" said Mrs. Brown in tones of relief. "Anyway, at least we know Henry's present works."

"Even if Paddington's doesn't," said Judy. "Perhaps they'll change it for you if you take it back to the shop," she added, catching sight of the disappointed look on his face as he clambered back down the ladder.

"It's a bit difficult with paws," said Paddington sadly as he tested the lock. For some reason or other it seemed to have jammed shut again. He glanced hopefully at the Sauna hut. "Perhaps my pores need opening?"

"Pores nothing!" broke in Jonathan. "What date did you say you used?"

"My birthday date," replied Paddington. "June the twenty-fifth."

"That's your summer one," said Jonathan. "You want

to try the winter one next time. *December* the twenty-fifth." And to prove his point he took the lock from Paddington, twiddled the dials, and then opened and closed it several times in quick succession.

"I always knew there must be something against having two birthdays a year," said Mrs. Brown. "Now I know. Life must be very confusing sometimes—especially if you're a bear."

"Especially," agreed Paddington, "if you're a bear with combinations."

CHAPTER SEVEN

Pantomime Time

THE BROWNS EXCHANGED GLANCES as they pushed their way through the crowds thronging the street outside the Alhambra Theatre.

While Judy took a firm grip of Paddington's left paw, Mrs. Bird clasped her umbrella and took up station on his other side.

"Don't let go of my hand whatever you do," said Judy. "We don't want you to get lost."

"And watch your hat," warned Mrs. Bird. "If it gets knocked off and trampled underfoot you may never see it again."

Paddington needed no second bidding, and with his other paw he placed his suitcase firmly on top of his head.

It was the start of the pantomime season in London and as a special Christmas treat Mr. Brown had reserved seats for the opening night of *Dick Whittington*.

It was a long time since Paddington had been taken to a theater, and he'd certainly never ever been to a pantomime before, so he was very much looking forward to the occasion.

Mr. Gruber, who'd also been included in the party, brought up the rear, and as they made their way up the steps he tapped Paddington on the shoulder and motioned him to listen to an announcement coming through on a loudspeaker. It was all about the dangers of buying souvenir programs from unauthorized sellers outside the theater who were apparently charging no less than two pounds a time.

Paddington could hardly believe his ears and he gave one man, wearing an old raincoat, a very hard stare indeed from beneath his suitcase as a brightly colored booklet was thrust under his nose

"*Two pounds* for a program!" he exclaimed.

"I've never heard of such a thing!" agreed Mrs. Bird, poking the man menacingly with her umbrella.

The man gave them a nasty look. "Just you wait," he

said. "Some people don't know when they're well off."

"I wonder what he meant by that?" asked Mr. Brown, as they reached the entrance doors at long last.

Paddington didn't know either, but before he had time to consider the matter he found himself being addressed by a superior-looking official standing inside the foyer.

"Good for you," said the man approvingly. "I wish more of our patrons took such a firm line with these people. It's costing us a small fortune in lost sales. Allow me to offer you one of our official programs."

"Thank you very much," said Paddington gratefully. "I'll have seven, please."

"*Seven!*" The man looked even more impressed as he signaled one of the usherettes to join them.

"Seven of our special souvenir programs for the young bear gentleman, Mavis," he called.

"Thank you *very* much, sir," said the girl as she counted out the programs and handed them to Paddington. "That'll be twenty-one pounds, please."

"*Twenty-one pounds!*" exclaimed Paddington, nearly falling over backwards in alarm. "That's *three* pounds each. I wish I'd bought some outside now!"

Mr. Gruber gave a cough. "I think perhaps we'd better have one for you to keep, Mr. Brown," he said, before anyone else had time to speak. "And seven ordinary ones for the rest of us."

"*Seven*, Mr. Gruber?" echoed Judy. "Don't you mean six?"

"I expect young Mr. Brown would like to send one to his Aunt Lucy when he next writes," said Mr. Gruber. And ignoring the protests from the others he handed over the money. "It's my pleasure," he said. "I don't know when I last went to a pantomime."

After thanking Mr. Gruber for his kind act, Paddington gave the staff in the foyer some very dark glances indeed as they went on their way. They suggested he was going to have a great deal to say on the subject of theaters when he next wrote to his aunt. In fact, it was going to take a very large postcard indeed to get it all in.

But as they took their seats in the front row of the stalls and he examined his program, Paddington began to cheer up again, for it was full of colored pictures with lots of reading as well, and despite the high cost the more he looked at it the better value it seemed.

"That's a picture of the Principal Boy," explained Judy, as she caught a puzzled look on his face. "It's being played by a girl."

"The Dame's played by a man," broke in Jonathan.

If they thought their explanations were going to help Paddington's understanding of pantomimes they were mistaken.

"Why don't they change over?" he asked. "Then everything would be all right."

"They can't," said Jonathan. "The Dame's *always* played by a man."

"And the Principal Boy is *always* a girl," agreed Judy. "It's traditional."

"I don't see why," insisted Paddington.

The others lapsed into silence. Now that Paddington mentioned it, they couldn't think of a very good reason either, but luckily the orchestra chose that moment to launch into the overture and so the subject was dropped for the time being.

Mrs. Brown glanced along the row. "Don't miss the opening scene, dear," she called. "You'll see Dick Whittington's marmalade cat."

Paddington licked his lips. "I shall enjoy that, Mrs. Brown," he announced.

The Browns looked at each other uneasily. "Well . . ." began Mr. Brown. "Don't be too disappointed. It isn't a *real* cat."

"I shouldn't think so," said Paddington. "Not if it's made of marmalade."

"It isn't actually *made* of marmalade either," said Judy.

"Besides, it's in two parts," remarked Jonathan.

"Dick Whittington's cat's in two parts!" exclaimed Paddington. He jumped up from his seat in order to consult his program. Once, when he'd been taken to the theater there had been a small slip tucked inside saying that one of the actors was indisposed, but either words had failed the management on this occasion, or they were keeping the matter very dark, for no matter how hard he shook his program nothing fell out.

"I didn't mean the *cat* was in two parts," hissed Jonathan as the house lights dimmed. "I meant two people take turns to play it."

"It's hard work," said Judy. "It gets very hot inside the fur."

"I get very hot inside *my* fur sometimes," said Paddington severely, "but there's only one of me."

Judy gave a sigh. Paddington was inclined to take things literally and sometimes it was difficult explaining matters to him, but fortunately she was saved any further complications as the curtain rose to reveal the street outside the home of the famous London shipping merchant, Alderman Fitzwarren.

The Browns settled back to enjoy the show and as the cast went into the opening chorus even Paddington seemed to forget the problem.

He cheered loudly when Dick Whittington arrived on the scene with Sukie, the cat, and when both Dick and Sukie collapsed on the steps of Alderman Fitzwarren's house, faint with hunger, it was with difficulty that the Browns managed to restrain him from going up on stage.

"I don't think a marmalade sandwich would help, dear," whispered Mrs. Brown nervously, as Paddington began feeling inside his hat.

"It happens every night," hissed Mr. Brown.

"Twice nightly on Thursdays and Saturdays," agreed Jonathan.

Paddington fell back into his seat. He found it hard to

picture anyone going without food at the best of times, let alone twice nightly on Thursdays and Saturdays, and having already removed the marmalade sandwich from under his hat he decided to make the most of it.

For the rest of the first act, apart from a few boos at appropriate moments, much to everyone's relief the only sound to be heard from Paddington's direction was that of a steady munching as he polished off the remains of his emergency supply.

During the interval, while Mr. Brown went to fetch some ice-cream, Mr. Gruber attempted to explain some of the plot to Paddington.

"You see, Mr. Brown," he said, "Dick Whittington came to London because he thought the streets were paved with gold, but like many others before him he soon found his mistake. Luckily, he was taken in by Alderman Fitzwarren—rather like Mr. and Mrs. Brown took you in when they found you on Paddington Station. Alderman Fitzwarren was so pleased at the way Sukie drove off all the rats in his house, that when he sent one of his ships to the West Indies he let Dick and Sukie go along too."

"The second half is all about how they land on the Boko Islands and how Sukie saves the day there," said Judy.

"There's a magic act as well," broke in Jonathan, reading from his program. "He's called the 'Great Divide.'"

Paddington pricked up his ears as he polished off the remains of his ice-cream. He was keen on conjuring and, all in all, now that he'd got over his first confusion, he decided he liked pantomimes. There was a bit too much singing and dancing for his taste, but some of the scenery was very good indeed, and he applauded to no end when Dick and Sukie arrived on the island and in the excitement of a quick change one of the stage hands got left on stage by mistake.

But he reserved his best claps for the moment when a black velvet cloth came down and in the glow of a single spotlight the majestic figure of the magician, resplendent in top hat and a flowing black cape, strode on to the stage.

After removing several rabbits and a goldfish bowl from his hat, and a seemingly endless string of flags of all nations from his left ear, the Great Divide came forward to address the audience, while behind him several girls in tights and gold costumes wheeled on an assortment of mysterious-looking boxes.

"And now," he said, silencing a drum roll with his hand, "I would like one volunteer from the audience."

"Oh, dear, Henry," said Mrs. Brown, as there was a

sudden flurry of movement from alongside them. "I knew it was a mistake to sit in the front row."

"Trust Paddington," agreed Jonathan.

"How was I to know this would happen?" said Mr. Brown unhappily.

The Browns watched anxiously as Paddington clambered on to the stage carrying his suitcase. But if the Great Divide was at all taken aback he managed to hide his feelings remarkably well, and after some more chit-chat he opened one of the boxes with a flourish and motioned Paddington to sit inside.

"I don't think I've ever sawn a bear in two before," he said, as he snapped the box shut.

"What!" exclaimed Paddington in alarm. "You're going to saw me in two!"

"They don't call me the Great Divide for nothing," chuckled the magician in an aside to the audience.

"You'd better watch the toggles on your duffle coat," he warned, as an assistant handed over one of the largest saws Paddington had ever seen and he pinged it with his finger to show it was genuine. "We don't want any trouble with splinters. I don't think there's a doctor on the island."

"Oh, dear," said Mrs. Brown nervously. "I hope he *doesn't* damage Paddington's coat—we shall never hear the last of it if he does."

"It's not that bear's *coat* I'm worried about," said Mrs. Bird grimly.

The Browns watched in silent fascination as the Great Divide placed his saw in a groove and began moving it rapidly to and fro in time to the Tritsch Tratsch Polka.

Although they knew nothing could possibly go wrong, the sound of metal going through wood seemed all too realistic. Their sighs of relief as the trick finally came to an end were matched only by Paddington's as he staggered round the stage feeling himself carefully in order to make sure he was still in one piece.

"And now"—once again the Great Divide raised his hand for silence—"as you have been such a good assistant, I'm going to make you disappear."

"Thank you very much," said Paddington gratefully.

He turned to leave, but before he had time to gather his wits about him he found himself being led into an even larger box. A moment later, as the doors slammed shut, he felt himself start to whirl round and round with ever-increasing speed as the magician began turning it on its wheels and the music rose to a crescendo.

A round of applause greeted the Great Divide as he brought the box to a stop and then opened up the doors in order to demonstrate how empty it was.

"Don't worry," said Mr. Gruber, as he caught sight of the look on Judy's face. "It's all done by mirrors. I'm sure young Mr. Brown will be all right."

As if to prove his statement, there came a loud knocking from somewhere on stage. "Let me out!" cried a muffled voice. "It's all dark."

Almost immediately the Great Divide abandoned his intention of producing some more rabbits out of thin air. He gave his assistants a quick glance of warning and hastily closed the cabinet doors. After twirling it round several more times he brought it to a stop again and reopened the doors.

The applause as Paddington staggered out on to the stage was even louder than it had been for the first trick.

"There, now," said the magician. "That wasn't so bad, was it? Tell everyone you are all right."

"I'm *not*," said Paddington, looking most upset. "I feel sick and I've lost my suitcase."

"You've lost your *what*?" repeated the Great Divide.

"My suitcase," said Paddington. "It's got all my important things inside it. I had it with me when I went inside your box—now it's disappeared."

The Great Divide's smile became even more fixed. For a moment or two he looked as if he was about to do a variation of his earlier trick, this time sawing Paddington not only in two, but into as many pieces as possible.

"Fancy taking a suitcase with you," he hissed, as he closed the doors once again. "In all my years on the stage I've never had this happen to me before."

"We'd better make sure everything's still in there," he continued sarcastically, as he re-did the trick, and after removing Paddington's suitcase from the box, opened it up in order to show the audience.

But as the Great Divide shook the case and nothing fell out his face fell. "I thought you said it was full of things," he exclaimed.

"It is, Mr. Divide," said Paddington firmly. "I'll show you." And taking his suitcase from the magician he turned his back and began feeling in the secret compartment.

"That's a photograph of my Aunt Lucy," he announced, waving a postcard in the air. "And that's my passport. Then there's my savings. And that's a map of

the Portobello Road . . . and a photograph I took with my camera . . . and my opera glasses . . . and a marmalade chunk . . . and . . ."

The rest of Paddington's remarks were lost in the storm of applause which rang out from all directions as object after object landed at the feet of the Great Divide.

"Bravo!" shouted someone sitting near the Browns. "Best double act I've seen in years."

"Had me fooled," agreed someone else nearby. "I thought it was just someone ordinary from the audience."

"Ordinary!" Mrs. Bird turned and fixed her gaze on the speaker. "Whatever else he is, Paddington certainly isn't *ordinary*. That's the last thing he is.

"Mind you," she remarked, as she settled back in her seat again while Paddington and his belongings were helped off the stage, "I always knew he kept a lot of things in that case of his, but I never dreamed he had quite so much."

After Paddington's appearance the rest of the pantomime seemed almost tame by comparison, although it soon picked up again and by the time Dick Whittington and Sukie arrived back in England, triumphant after their long voyage, Paddington was already safely in his seat and joining in the choruses. In fact, when Dick asked Alderman Fitzwarren for his daughter's hand in marriage and the news was given out that he would soon become Lord Mayor of London, he nearly lost his hat in the general excitement.

When the curtain finally came down some envious glances were cast in the Browns' direction as they were ushered backstage in order to meet the cast. Several people stopped Paddington and asked for his autograph, and he added his special paw-print to show that it was genuine.

"I hope you'll be very happy, Miss Whittington," he said, as they had their photograph taken together.

"I don't know about Dick Whittington being happy," said the manager. "I certainly am. This picture is going straight into our souvenir program. It'll make it even better value than ever and it'll teach those rascals outside a thing or two."

Even the Great Divide came out of his dressing-room to say goodbye, and to mark the occasion he presented Paddington with one of his magic saws.

It was a happy party of Browns who eventually climbed into the car for the journey home. To round things off Mr. Brown drove through the center of London so that they could see the Christmas lights, and then on to Westminster Abbey where Mr. Gruber pointed out a stained-glass window which showed a picture of Dick Whittington's cat.

But as they turned for home Paddington grew more and more thoughtful.

"Is anything the matter?" asked Mrs. Brown.

Paddington hesitated. "I was wondering if anyone had a large wooden box they don't want," he said hopefully.

"A large wooden box?" repeated Mr. Brown. "Whatever do you want that for?"

"I think I can guess," said Mrs. Bird, with a wisdom

born of long experience of reading Paddington's mind. "And the answer is 'no.'"

"I don't begrudge people their pleasures," she added, as they turned a corner into Windsor Gardens and she picked up Paddington's present from the Great Divide. "But I am not having anyone sawn in two in our house, thank you very much. Least of all a certain bear."

"I quite agree," said Mr. Gruber. "After all, Mr. Brown," he added, with a twinkle in his eye, "there's a lot of truth in the old saying 'two's company, three's a crowd.' If there were two of you I might have trouble sharing out our elevenses in future, and I wouldn't want that to happen—not for all the cocoa in the world."